BOOK OF NO SLEEP

無眠書2

點子出版
IDEA PUBLICATION

哈囉！各位讀者你們好嗎？看完《無眠書》之後，還睡得安穩嗎？

《無眠書2》比上集少了奇幻、預測未來等等較抽象的故事，這次的故事多了現實性，**彷彿就在你身邊發生而你懵然不知**。我自己本身很喜歡看懸疑電影和詭異漫畫，所以希望能藉著《無眠書》系列把不安的感覺帶給讀者，讓更多人也能欣賞並享受這類作品，更希望你們會喜歡翻譯文學。

雖然古語有云：「平生不作虧心事，夜半敲門也不驚。」但當人類看見或想到有可怕事情的時候，仍是會激發恐懼的本能。就如有一次，我在夜裏聽見樓上傳來「咚咚」聲，本來只是覺得是鄰居在切肉做飯而已，沒甚麼大不了。但腦海突然飄過一個想法——*「你已經成為一宗肢解案的重要證人了」*，不禁打了個哆嗦。

人類的心理很奇怪，你愈是急著不要去想讓自己害怕的情節，卻愈是會在腦海裏重複出現，揮之不去。但這種不安感卻是驚慄小說作家的泉源，有些故事甚至取材自真實兇案。

單單是香港，在 2007 年至 2017 年間，平均每個月就有約二十宗兇殺案，當中有些是尚未破解的懸案。我相信除了這些有紀錄的案件之外，一定還有未被報導、犯人消遙法外的案件，而且為數不少。香港地小人多，*兇手會否曾經與你擦身而過，又會否是我們認識的人？*

近年廣為人知的例子有 2008 年的王嘉梅命案、2013 年的大角咀肢解父母案、2016 年的油麻地碧街便利店命案，還有剛剛在 2018 年 1 月發生的屯門父母虐女致死案。這些兇手跟受害者可能互不相識，只是遇上無妄之災而不幸身亡；但兇手也有可能是死者的親生父母、親生子女，叫人**防不勝防**。

今集所精選的 70 篇故事，很少著墨妖魔鬼怪的恐怖，反而更多描寫人性黑暗面，完美演繹了人與人之間信任的脆弱。讀者們看故事的時候不妨代入不同角色，試試揣摩他們的心理和邏輯吧！

看過這些故事後，你再想想，是非黑白、對錯善惡，又是否有清晰的界線呢？

陳婉婷

CONTENTS
目 錄

死亡真相 Miserable Truth

Look at Me
天台的瘋子 12

The Sound of Silence
寂靜之聲 14

A Better Place
安息 15

Can I Come Inside?
迷途小男孩 17

Under the Covers
救命被單 19

Virus
病毒 20

Bloody Mary is a Bitch
婊子血腥瑪莉 22

I Really Don't Drink Much
酒後亂性 25

The Sound of Screaming was
Drowned Out by Laughter,
Then a Chainsaw
先是尖叫聲,然後是笑聲,
再來是電鋸聲 27

You Know the Deal
夢想成真 29

Rolling in Their Graves
掘屍真相 31

The Cure for Cancer
癌症治療 33

I was on a Reality Dating Show
約會真人秀 35

Little Bastard
混蛋小孩 37

Meeting Death
遇見死神 40

Sympathy Pains
擬娩症候群 43

All Watered Down
全都稀釋掉 45

Desert Roads
沙漠公路 48

Julia was a Very Bad Girl
壞女孩 Julia 50

Please Ignore My Suicide
請無視我的自殺 52

Erotomania
情愛妄想症 54

Howdy Neighbor Days
鄰里同樂節 57

The Twins
雙生兒 59

Fun With 911
報案室奇趣錄 61

My Daughter is a Sensitive Child
睡前故事 65

The Recognition He Deserved
好朋友的承諾 67

He is Coming Again
他又來了 70

辣手報復 Vicious Revenge

Natural Born Killer
天生殺人狂 75

Mandatory Euthanasia
強制性安樂死 76

A Good Wife
賢妻 78

It's a Small Town
小鎮大事 80

They Called Me Elephant Man
我不是象人 83

You Never Call, You Never Write...
音訊全無 85

Not Like Other Girls
不像其他女生 87

A Mother's Love
母親的愛 90

I Did All I Could
我已竭盡所能 93

I'm a Very Good Husband
廿四孝丈夫 96

Not the Worst Way to Die
不算最慘的死法 99

gluttonygreedslothlustprideenvy
WRATH
七宗罪之憤怒 101

It's Common for People
to Undergo a Personality Change
after Brain Trauma
腦外傷後人格劇變的
現象很普遍 103

The Scarecrow
稻草人 126

My Sister's Hogging
the Bathroom Again
姊姊又佔著浴室了 128

無情背叛 Ruthless Betrayal

At Least We Have Each Other
相依為命 107

Caught in Traffic
少女拍賣會 110

Katie
私奔 113

I Love My Wife
愛妻心切 115

Just for a Moment
紋身的故事 116

Children Should Be Seen and
Not Heard
孩子安靜才乖 119

My Boyfriend Has a Weird Obsession
男朋友的怪癖 121

I'm a Very Good Girl
我是個乖女兒 124

困境抉擇 Wretched Dilemma

The Choice
抉擇 132

The Worst Thing
最糟糕的事 135

A Day Off in Hell
地獄休息日 138

You Need to Eat
厭食症 141

The Beep Test
地獄式體能訓練 144

Poor Boys
避雨 146

But I'm Not Bitter
但我沒有不滿 148

Privatization
警力私有化 150

Emergency Eclipse Instructions
日食緊急指引 151

A Letter from the
Previous Homeowner
前屋主的信 153

極端妄想 Virulent Delusion

Baxter Didn't Recognize Me
Baxter 不認得我了 158

I'm Not Suicidal, I'm Just
Testing Her
隱形的自己 161

I Didn't Turn Up for
My Mother's Funeral
我缺席了母親的喪禮 164

My Daughter Never Ran Away
我女兒沒有離家出走 166

Dementia & Chopsticks
痴呆症與筷子 167

If You See Me, You Should
Probably Kill Me
請殺掉我 169

Home Alone
獨自在家 172

He Deserved to Die
他是該死的 173

A Game of Hide and Seek
捉迷藏 175

Tap Tap Tap
嗒嗒嗒 177

Miserable Truth
死 亡 真 相

Look at Me

Being hundreds of feet in the air is definitely dizzying. The fetid city air is only a faint perfume all the way up here. The breeze nearly knocks me over as I maneuver over the railing, almost ending my escapade in that instant. My bleached white shirt serves as a beacon to anyone willing to look up, not that the smog–filled sky is much to look at. But they do. One or two people stop at a time, wondering what they're looking at. I stand at attention as whispers and murmurs float up to my ears.

A crowd begins to form.

The realization sets in, and panic fills the crowd. I sway a little, just to add to the edge. I can hear them shouting at me. I can't understand what they're saying, but I know what they want: "Don't do it!" I'll have to disappoint them, though. Cop cars pull up, and in ten minutes there are cops on the roof. I lean forward slightly, and they get the message and back off.

For now. It's like glitter spilled on the ground; it's amazing how many people can forget to turn off the flash on their phone cameras. But it fades away. People are recording me now, waiting to see what I'll do next. An unpredictable, unstable mind like mine? I am now a topic of interest, the center of their attention. It's almost euphoric. For once in my

天台的瘋子

站在離地數百呎的高空，難免會感到頭暈目眩。本來城市裏發臭的空氣，在這裏變成了淡淡幽香。在我跨越欄杆之際，一陣清風差點就把我吹倒，幾乎馬上就結束了我這個冒險行為。在這個煙霧彌漫、沒有甚麼好看的天空裏，身上潔白的袖衫使我像個燈塔般，照耀著那些願意抬頭望上來的人們。有一兩個人停下來，看看那些人在看甚麼。他們的悄悄話和呢喃聲傳到我的耳中，使我站直了身子。

人們開始聚集起來。

當那些群眾察覺到我想做甚麼時，他們都非常恐慌。我有點動搖，但是那種動搖卻讓我更想快點行動。我聽見他們向我叫喊著，雖然我聽不懂他們在說甚麼，但我知道他們在表達：「不要這樣做！」的意思，可是我將會令他們失望了。警車駛至，十分鐘後警察就到達了天台。我把身體稍微向前傾，他們明白我的意思，然後退後了。

現在這個畫面就像閃粉灑滿了一地，竟然有那麼多人用電話拍照時忘記關掉閃光燈呢！那些光點逐漸消失，換成了在錄影，期待著我這個既反覆無常，又心浮氣躁的瘋子下一步會幹甚麼。我現在成了他們議論紛紛的話題人物，全部人都很關注我！我很亢奮，因為這是我生平第一次，有人會在乎我將作出的決定。那我還在等甚麼？問得好。

life, people are concerned about the decisions I'll make. So, what am I waiting for? Excellent question.

One of the cops approaches me slowly. "Sir, please, you don't have to do this." Another one yells, "Don't you dare!" And there it is. A life hangs in the balance, and they're desperate now, I can tell. Now is the time to give my audience a show.

My fingers loosen, and the woman shakes her head furiously behind her gag, tears streaming down her face. A wicked grin dances across my lips, and I let her topple forward. The screams from below rise to a satisfying crescendo as her body hits the concrete, spraying blood everywhere. Even up here I can see the stain.

Shock, disbelief, horror. They stare at me, the monster above.

其中一個警察慢慢向我走近，勸道：「先生，請你不要這樣做。」另一個警察則大叫道：「你有種就試試看！」那好吧，現在命懸一線，我看得出來他們很絕望。現在就讓我給觀眾表演一番吧。

我鬆開了手，那個嘴巴被堵住的女人猛地搖頭，淚流滿面。我咧嘴一笑，然後把搖搖欲墜的她推向前方。她的身軀撞上地面的混凝土後，尖叫聲從下面漸強地傳上來，血液也噴得到處也是，就連我站在這裏也能看到。

群眾帶著震驚、難以置信和恐懼的表情抬頭看，看著我這個怪物。

The Sound of Silence

After lifetime of being deaf, my best friend just received cochlear implants. When he woke up from the surgery, we all stood around him. His wife was the first one to say anything. He heard her voice and at once began to cry. We all took turns speaking, letting him hear our voices and our names, and with each word we said, he became more emotional. When we were all finished, silence hung in the room.

He looked up at me and asked what that sound was. It took me a moment to understand what he was hearing, and when I understood, I told him he was hearing silence.

He shook his head. "This isn't silence," he said slowly, hearing his own voice for the first time. "I've been hearing silence all my life, and this is different."

A sound came from just outside the hospital room, and he perked up immediately. "Isn't that silence?"

We all exchanged looks of trepidation around the room before I spoke.

"No," I said slowly. "That was the sound of someone screaming."

寂靜之聲

我的好朋友天生是個聾子，他剛剛完成了人工耳蝸植入手術。他術後醒過來時，我們都站在他身邊。第一個跟他說話的是他的妻子，他聽見了妻子的聲音，感動得不禁哭了起來。然後我們每個人輪流跟他說話，讓他聽見我們的聲音和名字。他聽見我們每說出一個字，他就愈激動。我們都說完了之後，房間只剩一片寧靜。

他望著我，問我這是甚麼聲音。我想了一會，才意識到他聽見的聲音是甚麼，我回答說他聽見的是寧靜。

他搖搖頭：「這不是寧靜，」他緩緩地說著，那是他第一次聽見自己的聲音，「我一生以來都聽著寧靜，它不是這樣的。」

病房外傳來一下聲音，他立刻抖擻起來：「那不就是寧靜嗎？」

在我開口之前，房裏的眾人都惶恐不安地交換著眼色。

「不是，」我緩緩地說：「那是有人尖叫的聲音。」

A Better Place

"This must be so hard," they all said. Or something like that. Condolences.

No shit. I stared at her coffin, a deep red mahogany that contrasted with the muddy brown of the dirt in the hole. Six feet under.

The funeral service was fine. What do you expect me to say? Someone you loved dearly, Dead. Never to speak to you again. Never hearing your voice again.

I refused to speak at the service. I just sat and stared at her coffin in the ground. People cried. Her family, my family, her friends. I didn't cry. Shock had already passed over me but it was gone. I stood emotionless. The only thing that jolted me back to the present was the thumping sounds of piles of dirt falling into the grave.

People left. One by one. I stood by the gravesite. Everyone understood. He wants one last moment with her.

They didn't understand. They didn't even know.

安息

「他一定很難過吧……」他們都這樣說，或是説著類似的話，慰問著我。

少廢話吧。我凝望著她的棺材，在六呎荒土之下，桃木的深紅色與坑裏泥土的啡色形成對比。

葬禮儀式服務一切安好。你還期望我會説甚麼嗎？你深愛的那個人死掉了，不會再跟你説話，也不會再聽見你的聲音了。

我在葬禮上沒有説話，只是靜靜坐著，盯著她那埋在地下的棺材。她的家人、我的家人、她的朋友，所有人都在哭。但我沒有哭，我曾經很震驚，但那種感覺已經消逝了。我只是木無表情地站著。唯一把我從呆滯拉回現實世界的，是那些泥土掉落在棺材上的呼呼聲。

人們一個接一個地離開，我依舊站在墓前。他們都懂，認為我想陪她度過最後一刻。

他們其實不懂，他們根本就不知道。

I'd already had my last moment with her. It was when I wrapped my hands around her throat and squeezed the life out of her. And I'd have many other moments to come with her.

Another person, grimly, patted my shoulder and said "I'm so sorry. But she's in another place now. A better place."

She wasn't in a better place. She wasn't even in her coffin.

She was in my closet.

我早已陪她度過了最後一刻。那時候，我用雙手纏著她的脖子，親手榨乾了她的生命。而且我將會有更多跟她一起度過的時刻呢！

又有一個人冷冷地拍拍我的肩膀跟我說：「我很遺憾，但她現在到了另一個地方，一個更好的地方。」

她不在更好的地方，甚至不在她的棺材裏。

她在我的衣櫃裏。

Can I Come Inside?

Sometimes they come in the form of a lost child, other times, they come looking for a phone because their car broke down, but they always ask the same question. *"Can I come inside? It won't take long."*

I first met one when I was a child. I was home alone, my mother having gone to the store for an hour or so, and a woman holding a baby knocked on the door. She told me that her car broke down and that she needed to call her husband. It was hot outside – really hot – and I remember thinking it was weird that the baby was bundled up in a blanket and not crying, and even stranger still that I didn't see any car outside.

I told her no, and closed the door. She didn't knock again.

Although I wouldn't make the connection until nearly a decade later, I heard a story on the news that evening of a family disappearing from their home. There were no signs of a struggle, no signs of violent entry, and no signs of packing. They had simply just vanished.

Yesterday, I had a little boy come to my door. He was crying and told me he lost his mom and needed to come inside. He was about six perhaps, but when I asked him where he lived, he didn't respond. He just said. *"Please can I come inside? It won't take long."*

迷途小男孩

有時候他們會扮成迷路的小孩，有時又會「因為車子拋錨了所以過來借電話」，但他們一定會問這個問題：「*可以讓我進來嗎？我不會耽誤你很久的。*」

第一次遇到他們時，我還只是個小孩子。當時只有我一個人在家，媽媽去了商店買東西，離開了一個多小時。有個抱著嬰兒的女人走過來敲門，跟我說她的車子拋錨了，所以想借電話打給丈夫。現在回想起來真奇怪，那時天氣明明很熱，真的很熱，但她懷裏的寶寶卻裏著毯子，也沒有哭鬧。更讓我覺得詭異的是，外面一輛車子也沒有。

我拒絕了她，然後關上了門。她也沒有再敲門了。

雖然隨後差不多十年我再沒有遇見過他們，但我在新聞看到，有個家庭一夜之間消失了。沒有打鬥、強行闖入的痕跡，也沒有收拾行李的徵兆，就是突然消失了。

昨天，有個小男孩走到我的門前，他哭著跟我說他和媽媽走失了，想進來我家。他大概六歲左右吧，但當我問他住在哪裏時，他沒有回答我，他只是說：「*拜託你，可以讓我進來嗎？我不會耽誤你很久的。*」

That sentence sparked a connection in my brain that took me back to when I was a child and the woman with the baby, and the disappearance of the family down the street. Word for word, he'd said the exact same thing she had: *Can I come inside? It won't take long.*

Against my better judgement, I told him no and closed the door. There were other houses he could go to – mine is by far not the only house on the street – but something inside the instinctual part of my brain told me that I needed to close the door.

An hour ago, on the news, I watched a story about a family that had seemingly disappeared from their home. Their car was still in the driveway, there was no sign of struggle or forced entry. The front door was left open and the phone was off the hook. The only clue the police had to go on was a hastily written message in the corner of the wall: ***DON'T LET THEM INSIDE.***

那句說話刺激了我的腦海，讓我回想起小時候那個抱著嬰兒的女人，還有憑空消失了的那一家人……他一字不漏的說著跟那個女人一樣的話：「*可以讓我進來嗎？我不會耽誤你很久的。*」

我違心地拒絕了他，然後關上了門。我腦袋的本能反應驅使我把他拒諸門外，並安慰著自己道：「他還有其他房子可以去啊，我的家又不是這條街上唯一一間房子。」

一個小時之前，我在新聞看到又有一家人離奇失蹤了。他們的車子還在車道上，沒有任何打鬥或強行闖入的痕跡。他們的前門打開了，電話懸垂著。警察能追查的唯一線索，是寫在牆角落的潦草字跡：***不要讓他們進來。***

Under The Covers

When Adam was little, he used to click off the lights to his bedroom and sprint to his bed as quickly as he could every night.

He would fly over toys and stub his toes, but that never mattered; what mattered was getting to the safety of his covers before the things that live in the dark could get him.

He imagined twisted hands and claws and teeth coming out from the darkness, reaching for him as he ran, abated only by his bed and the protective shell he made around himself with the bedsheets.

When the things in the dark finally came for him, taking the form of a man climbing through the window, he thought that it was the covers that saved his life.

Instead, he was saved by the simple fact that his little brother wasn't quite as fast.

救命被單

當 Adam 還小的時候，每次他把睡房燈關掉之後，就會馬上飛奔到自己的床上，每晚如是。

他會在玩具堆中左穿右插，有時更會碰傷腳趾頭，但那都不要緊。最重要是在那些活在黑暗中的怪物抓到自己之前，可以安全躲進被窩裏就行了。

Adam 幻想那些黑暗中的怪物有著扭曲變形的手、長著爪子和尖牙，在他逃跑的同時會追著他，而他的床和被單就是他的防護罩，可以保護他不受怪物襲擊。

那些怪物終於來到他面前，準備抓走他，但它突然變成了一個男人的模樣，從窗口爬了出去。Adam 以為是被單保護了自己，救了自己的命。

但其實，他能活下來的原因很簡單——弟弟跑得不夠快。

Virus

I stood just outside of the swarm of people, safe in my hazmat suit. Hundreds of medical professionals flitted from patient to patient, taking note of vitals and basic condition. I felt useless, not knowing exactly what to do except count, and I'd long ago finished that task.

100,000.

100,000 people infected and detained within a single night. It was amazing and terrifying and disgusting and horrifying.

The virus had crept from bites of unknown origin and effectively covered the entirety of the skin tissue in a sick crimson. I secretly dubbed the patients "red people." The color was unnatural, like paint, but of course I wasn't about to test the texture.

The patients lay, moaning, skin practically steaming from the intense fevers. I could feel myself shivering from the sight of so many people in suffering. In my daze, I didn't notice a panicked doctor rushing in my direction, and he clearly didn't notice me. We collided, and he muttered a quick apology before scooping up the now tainted instruments.

病毒

我站在人群外面，穿著保護衣的我很安全。看著數以百計的醫護人員，在眾多病人之間來回穿梭，替病人摘錄著重要資料，以及基本的身體狀況。我覺得自己很沒用，除了數數之外，不知道還有甚麼可以幫忙，而且我早就已經數完了。

十萬。

一夜之間有十萬個病人受到感染，而且被拘留在此。這件事又有趣，又震驚，又厭惡，又可怕。

那是一種由未知來源的病毒引起的傳染病，會經由叮咬傳播。感染後病毒會完全覆蓋患者全身皮膚組織，使皮膚變成深紅色。我暗地裏把那些病患稱作「紅人」，那種顏色很不自然，看起來像是油漆般。但我不打算摸摸看那會是甚麼質感。

那些病人躺在病床呻吟著，發高燒使他們的皮膚滾燙得快要冒出蒸氣。看著這麼多人被病毒折磨，我也不禁顫抖了起來。我看得入神，沒有注意到有個醫生正慌忙地衝向我這邊，而他也沒有看到我。於是我們撞個正著，他呢喃著道歉的說話，然後匆匆地把那些受污染的工具撿起來。

There were bloodstains on the floor, no doubt from some type of blood test. The sample was everywhere. A cleaner quickly swept in to address the issue.

Unnerved, I wove through the countless tents of people, wanting to turn in my report and leave. Seeing all that red... I trembled. Seeing all the blood and pus and sweat... I swore I could feel a damp spot on my arm. Rubbing at it, I felt cool air rush in.

My suit was cut.

What's more, my *skin* was cut.

I tried to control my breathing, but I could already feel something creeping, shrouding me. More faces gradually turned my way. A soldier, suited as well, aimed a gun at me, and I halted in compliance. There was nothing to do. In the scarlet dawn, I could spy a faint difference in my reflection in the bulky goggles. I did my job, and counted.

100,001.

地上有些血跡，想必是一些用來做測試的血液樣本吧。摔破了的血液樣本弄得到處也是，很快就有一名清潔工過來把地下擦乾淨了。

我很不安，穿越了在無數個臨時帳篷，很想快點交完報告，快點離開這裏。看著一片緋紅，我不禁顫抖起來……看著那些血液、膿汁、汗水……看著看著，我彷彿感到自己的手臂也是濕答答的。我揉了揉手臂，感覺到有冷空氣溜到保護衣裏面……

我的保護衣被割破了。

更可怕的是，我的皮膚被割破了。

我盡量控制呼吸，但已經有種毛骨悚然的感覺正逐漸包圍著我。愈來愈多臉孔朝我看過來。一位同樣穿著保護衣的士兵舉起了槍瞄著我，我服從地停了下來。我已無能為力。紅霞漸降，我從厚重的護目鏡裏看到自己的倒影隱約有些不同了。盡責的我繼續數著數。

十萬零一。

Bloody Mary is a Bitch

"We should make my last day legendary," David told me with a smile. He hadn't told anyone else in the school that he was moving away in the middle of February. "What if everyone thought that Bloody Mary took me away?"

The plan was brilliant. After class, he and I would announce that we would summon the ghost in the mirror, and he'd slip out the window. It was a short reach down to the second–floor balcony, and he would climb onto it, sneak down the stairs, and walk home. I would come out and announce that Bloody Mary had taken him into the Other World, and no one would ever see him again.

There were at least two dozen people who gathered around on that Friday after school. David and I were barely able to contain our smirks as we went into the bathroom alone.

"You know, we should at least try it," I explained. "That way, we won't be lying when we say we attempted to 'bring forth the ghost.'"

He blanched just a little. "Um – okay, I suppose so."

I boldly stepped in front of the mirror. He tentatively stood next to me.

婊子血腥瑪莉

「我要把我在校的最後一天弄得與眾不同！」David 笑著說。他二月中就要搬家了，但他只跟我說過，其他同學還未知道。「不如讓他們以為是血腥瑪莉把我捉走了吧！」

我們的計劃很完美，我和 David 打算下課後宣佈，我們將從鏡子裏召喚出鬼魂，然後他就會從窗口爬到外面。那個窗口離二樓的露台很近，David 只須爬過去，然後偷偷跑下樓梯，就可以走回家了。待他跑掉了之後，我就會走出來，慌張地跟大家說，血腥瑪莉已經帶他到另一個世界，大家再也不會見到他了。

那天下課後，至少有二十幾個人聚集了起來，我和 David 兩人走進廁所後，就忍不住奸笑了起來。

「好吧，一於試試看吧。」我說：「這樣跟他們說我們嘗試『召出鬼魂』，就不會是說謊了。」

他明顯被我的話嚇倒了，臉色也蒼白了一點，「呃……那好吧，試試看吧。」

我大膽地站到鏡子前面，David 則躊躇地站到我旁邊。

"Bloody Mary, Bloody Mary, Bloody Mary – I killed your son." His voice echoed mine, albeit haltingly.

We stared into our reflections. We blinked. So did they.

Nothing happened.

We both let out a sigh of relief.

"I'd better get out of here," David offered. "It's time."

He put one leg up on the sink, and one on the open window, before offering me a last goodbye. "See ya," he said with a smile.

He looked down and shifted his weight in order to position himself for the window escape. He was halfway out when I decided that I couldn't resist.

"Boo!" I shouted at him as I jumped forward.

His eyes shot up immediately and betrayed a moment of terror.

Honestly, I hadn't meant to make him slip.

「血腥瑪莉，血腥瑪莉，血腥瑪莉，我殺了你的兒子。」雖然 David 結結巴巴的，但還是跟我一起唸出了召喚咒語。

我們凝視著自己的倒影。我們眨了眼，它們也眨了眼。

甚麼事也沒有發生。

我倆都鬆了一口氣。

「我還是先離開這裏吧，」David 提議，「時間差不多了。」

他一條腿踏著洗手盆，另一條腿跨出窗外。「拜拜。」他笑著跟我道別。

他望著下方，把重心移到另一邊，使他可以調整好爬出窗口的姿勢。當他半邊身都在窗外時，我按捺不住了。

「哇！」我向前跳，向他大叫了一聲。

他立刻望了上來，眼裏充滿恐懼。

老實說，我不是故意想他失足的。

David fell through the window and out of sight before I could react.

'Oh great,' I thought, 'now we'll have to deal with a twisted ankle.'

I walked over to the window and peaked my head through.

David's head was impaled, sideways, on a metal pole that had once been part of a chain–link fence. He must have fallen fifteen feet. It ran temple to temple. The top of the pole was coated in blood, and the tip of it had brain goop resting on it. His legs were twitching like he was running in place, but the pole held him firm. It wiggled as his legs danced.

His eyes never closed.

I think that Bloody Mary really did get us in the end.

At least, that's what I told everyone. I said that David got spooked at what he saw after the incantation, and jumped out the window.

And I see David's killer every time I look in the mirror.

在我反應過來之前，David 已經從窗口掉下去了，消失在我的視線範圍。

「這下好了，」我心想，「現在要處理扭傷的腳了。」

我走到窗邊，探頭望向下面。

David 掉下去的地方有一根鐵杆，那本來是鐵絲網圍欄的其中一部分。他從十五呎高的地方掉下去了，他的頭被鐵杆刺穿了，從一邊太陽穴穿到另一邊太陽穴。鐵杆的頂部染滿了血，末端還黏著一點腦漿。他的雙腳還在抽搐著，好像在跑步似的，但又被鐵杆牢牢抓住了般。他的腳抽動時，鐵杆也跟著搖晃。

他死不瞑目。

我想血腥瑪莉的詛咒最後真的靈驗了。

至少我跟其他人是這樣說的。我跟他們說 David 唸完咒語後看到了一些東西把他嚇壞了，然後就跳出窗口了。

而我，每次照鏡子都會看見殺死 David 的兇手。

I Really Don't Drink Much

"Come on, just one? One surely won't hurt you..." He's a good–looking guy, with arresting Celtic knotwork tattooed on his forearms, that makes her wonder, hazily, if the knotwork is all over him.

"I really don't drink much; I just don't handle alcohol well..."

"One little one?" he grins, engagingly. He really is quite attractive.

"I shouldn't...alcohol makes me—", but she takes it, anyway, and....

...And she is waking up, in her room. With a terrible headache.

Morning? What happened? Ooh, my head...

Her head and...

"Oh, God! Ummmmph——" she climbs stiffly out of bed and runs to the bathroom, her stomach heaving. She just makes it in time, and vomits violently into the toilet. She stands there a minute, shaking and dizzy, then heaves again. This time she is more aware of what she is throwing up, and how chunky, how wrong it feels.

酒後亂性

「來嘛，喝一杯吧？一杯不會很傷身的啦……」他是個帥哥，前臂有個凱爾特繩結紋身。這個紋身讓她在迷濛間猜想著他身上是不是也佈滿這樣的繩結呢？

「我真的不喝太多了，我醉了會很麻煩……」

「一小杯吧？」他展露著迷人的微笑，真的很吸引。
「不太好吧……喝酒會讓我……」但她還是喝了，然後……

然後她在自己的房間裏醒來，頭痛欲裂。

早上？發生甚麼事了？呃……我的頭……

她的頭還有……

「天啊！嘔唔……」她立即從床上飛奔到廁所，嘔吐大作。她剛好趕得及來到廁所，猛烈地嘔吐著。她站在旁邊休息了一分鐘，身體顫抖著，頭也很暈，然後又吐了一番。這次她才注意到她吐了甚麼出來、才注意到它們原來有多大塊，感覺有多不對勁。

Good God, what did I eat? She has only a vague memory of last night—a guy, a Celtic tattoo, but little else. "I tried to tell him I didn't drink...", but she can't recall anything else.

And then notices, though one tries not to look too closely, at just what she puked up...."What is...? That looks like...."

A—finger??

And chunks of——is that skin?

I must be hallucinating—she notices that one of the chunks has, undeniably, a piece of Celtic knotwork on it.... Snatches of last night are coming back now, and she stumbles wearily to the kitchen. It's happened again. There'll be a big mess to clean up, she knows.

After all, she knows *why* she doesn't drink much. She just doesn't handle alcohol well at all.

*我的天啊，我吃了甚麼啊？*她對昨晚的事記憶很模糊。只記得那個男生和那個凱爾特紋身，然後就沒有了。「我試著跟他說我不喝……」但其他的通通記不起。

雖然她不想細看她吐出來的東西，但還是注意到了。「甚麼來的？這看起來像是……」

手……手指？

那塊是……皮膚嗎？

*這肯定是幻覺……*她看到其中一塊嘔吐物上有著千真萬確的凱爾特繩結——昨晚的一點一滴像潮水般湧現，她拖住筋疲力盡的身軀走到廚房。那回事又再次發生了，她很清楚有很多麻煩要收拾處理。

她終於知道為*甚麼*她不能喝太多酒了，因為她醉了真的會很麻煩。

The Sound of Screaming was Drowned Out by Laughter, Then a Chainsaw

I lay on the road, looking up towards the sky. My voice was already hoarse from shouting; only the wisps of a broken heart remained in my whispers.

I clutched my old phone tightly, having sold my new one just hours ago. The only belongings I had left were the clothes on my back and this ancient cell. Were there any cars coming by? I sure hoped so.

The mountain looks pretty today. Maybe if I had the strength to scream, a boulder would fall on me. Maybe it'd just knock me out and I'd have to spend the rest of my life comatose.

Impossible, though. I can't afford it. My savings...

$30,000 in cash. It took several days and selling almost everything I had to acquire that sum of money. Even the sale of my caravan only gave me about $15,000 in cash. But I made it. I raised that sum of money, in hopes of securing a future.

But those bastards. The scoundrels who followed me from the bank, looking for an easy prey. I hope they never find happiness their entire lives, try as they might.

先是尖叫聲，然後是笑聲，再來是電鋸聲

我躺在路上，仰望著天空。我叫得嗓子都沙啞了，只能低聲說話的我，言語間只剩下心碎。

我緊握著一部老舊的電話，新的那部在幾個小時前被我賣掉了。我全副家當只剩下我身上的衣服，和這部老掉牙的手提電話。會有車子駛過這裏嗎？我當然希望有吧。

那座山今天看起來很美，如果我還有力氣尖聲大叫的話，可能會有大石頭掉下來砸中我；又如果那大石頭沒有把我砸死，那麼剩下的日子我就會在昏迷狀態中過活了。

但那是不可能的，我負擔不起，我的積蓄……

三萬美元現金，我用了好幾天時間，幾乎把所有東西都賣掉才籌到這筆錢。雖然那輛宿營拖車只賣得一萬五千多塊，但最後我還是籌到了。為了將來有一份保障，我籌了這筆錢。

但那些混蛋流氓，在我從銀行離開後一直跟蹤我，在他們眼中，我是隻很容易下手的獵物。我祝願他們無論怎麼努力也好，餘生也不會得到幸福。

My phone rings, jangling merrily. I raise it to my ears, praying with all my might.

"Why, hello there, Mrs Luthors!" came a cheerful, friendly voice. "I got your text. Did you really manage to raise the money?"

"Sto... Stolen..." I croaked.

The voice on the other end seemed to fret. "Oh no! That's terrible! Have you made a police report?"

Gathering all my strength, I whispered back, "No. Let... Let me..."

"Well, then." His voice grew stronger, sharper. "I will be generous to you, Mrs Luthors, considering you tried your hardest. This... wasn't part of the plan, let me assure you."

Hope filled my heart, and I sat up on the road, scrambling to the side. "What do you mean?!" I coughed, and tasted blood in my throat.

"I'll let you hear her last words."

我電話叮嚀嚀嚀地響起了。我把話筒放到耳邊，同時誠心祈禱著。

「噢，Luthors 太太你好！」話筒裏傳來一把歡愉又友善的聲音，「我收到你的短訊了，你真的籌到錢了嗎？」

「被⋯⋯被偷了⋯⋯」我沙啞地回答。

話筒裏的另一端似乎很擔心，「不是吧！太可怕了！你報警了嗎？」

儘管我花光所有力氣，都只能低聲回應他：「沒有，聽⋯⋯聽我⋯⋯」

「那好吧，」他聲線變得強硬了，「考慮到你已經盡了最大努力，我會對你仁慈一點的，Luthors 太太。不過，我先說清楚，這不是計劃的一部分喔。」

我頓時滿心歡喜，坐直了身子，爬向路邊。「那是甚麼意思？」我咳嗽著，嚐到了血的味道。

「我會讓你聽聽她的遺言。」

You Know the Deal

"You know the deal, three wishes, can't ask to be god, have unlimited wishes, etc,"

I frown, trying to comprehend the man that seemed to appear from thin air.

He rolls his eyes "I ain't got all day, 'urry up!"

"Y–yes, of course," I stammer, my palms sweaty, my ears growing red. "I wish that...my book is published and becomes more popular than Harry Potter!" I had always been a writer, struggling to look after my children and have a career, if my book sells, everything will work out.
"Very well," The man, or rather a Genie I guess you could call him, says "next one?"

"My wife! She died a few years back, it's impossible and–"
"Yadda, yadda, yadda," the Genie interrupts, "get to the point,"

"Bring her back, back to life,"
"Sure, whatever, next one?"

I think about this one more carefully. Usually, presented this situation, I would ask for multiple wishes, yet he's already ruled that out. And then I realize. I wish that will make all my

夢想成真

「你知道規矩的吧，三個願望，不可以要求做神，不可以要無限願望等等。」

望著從輕煙裏出現的男人，我皺起了眉頭，試著理解這到底是現實還是幻象。

他翻著白眼催促道：「不要浪費本大爺的時間，快點啦！」

「是……是的，知道了。」我結結巴巴地說。我緊張得手心冒汗，耳朵也通紅了。「我希望……我的書可以順利出版，而且會比《哈利波特》更加膾炙人口！」我是個作家，為了養活孩子，又要維持生計，一直在掙扎求存。如果我的書可以大賣，一切就不成問題了。

「很好，」那個男人，或者你們會叫他做燈神，問道：「第二個呢？」

「我太太！她前幾年過世了，這不可能的吧，但……」

「欸欸欸！」燈神打斷了我：「說重點。」

「讓她復活。」

「可以，隨你吧，最後一個呢？」

我仔細地想清楚最後一個願望。通常在這個情況下我會想多

wishes come true. Perfect.

It won't stop. The pain is endless. Day. Night. Everything. For everyone.

And it's all my fault. Each day is a new scenario. Somedays they are perfect, blissful. Yet that is rare. I can't die. I can't even escape this endless torment, nor can anyone else. It's just endless pain that leads to nothing.

See, my last wish was for all my dreams to come true. I forgot that most dreams are nightmares.

要幾個願望，但他已經說明了不可以，所以最後我希望我所有夢想都可以成真，這樣就完美了。

它不會停止，只有無窮無盡的痛苦……日復日，夜復夜……所有東西，所有人……

全部都是我的錯……每天都是一個新的場景，有些日子很完美、非常快樂，但很罕有。我無法死去，無法逃離這個無限的煉獄，其他人也無法逃脫。只剩無窮無盡的痛苦，只得一片虛無。

是的，我最後的願望是希望我所有「夢想」都可以成真，但我忘記了我大部分的夢都是惡夢……

Rolling in Their Graves

To whom it may concern,

I'm the one that's been desecrating the graves, digging up bodies in the middle of the night.

The cemetery owners have said many bad things about me on the news. I don't blame you for assuming the worst based on what you've heard. Six months ago, I would have been right there with you, thinking the same. But then I saw it for myself.

I swear to you, I never touched a single corpse. I am not a necrophiliac. I am not a Satanist. I am not a sick, twisted individual seeking to pain the relatives of the dead I have exposed.

Yes, I dug up a grave. Then another. Then another. I've lost count how many, perhaps two dozen, maybe three.

So what am I, if not any of those vile things?

I'm terrified.

The police want you to think that I'm the one who rearranged the bodies. I didn't. Not once, I swear!

掘屍真相

敬啟者：

最近一直在午夜褻瀆墳墓、把屍體掘出來的人是我。

那些墓地的持有人在報紙上說了很多關於我的壞話。如果你聽了他們的話後，設想了最糟狀況的話，我不會怪你。六個月前，我也跟你們有著一樣的想法。但直至我親眼目睹了事實，我就不再這樣想了。

我發誓，我以前從未接觸過任何屍體，我不是戀屍狂，也不是撒旦崇拜者，更不是個心理扭曲的變態，我把屍體掘出來也不是為了讓死者親屬陷入痛苦來滿足自己。

沒錯，我挖掘了一個墳墓，接著又挖了一個，然後又挖了另一個。我數不清自己挖了多少個，大概二十多個？也可能有三十個吧。

如果我不是上述那些變態，我還可以是甚麼？

我是個充滿恐懼的人。

警方想讓大家認為我就是那個翻亂屍體的人，但我沒有！一次也沒有，我發誓！

Each night, as I'm digging, I beg God to let this one be normal. "Please," I whisper, "be at rest, peaceful with eyes closed and hands clasped."

No one is listening.

For the last time, I swear I didn't touch any of them. I didn't turn them onto their stomachs. I didn't twist their necks backwards. I didn't distort their faces into the expression of pure horror. And I didn't claw at the bottom of the caskets.

I don't know when this began, but it's happening and it's happening everywhere. If you don't believe me, you can check for yourself. That's easy enough. You only need a shovel and time.

But time we might not have. If you can't understand why, you're not asking yourself the question that's been driving me to do the things I have done...

Tell me, if the dead are clawing their way down toward hell, what horror is coming for us from above?

我每一晚在挖掘的時候，都向上天祈求這次要是個正常的屍體。「拜託了，」我輕聲說：「拜託是個閉目、雙手握緊、安息的模樣吧。」

但神明沒有聽見我的禱告。

就在上一次挖掘……我發誓我真的沒有觸碰過他們！我沒有把他們翻過來，讓他們背部朝天；我沒有把他們的脖子扭到另一邊；我沒有扭曲他們的臉，使他們滿臉驚恐；那些棺木底部的抓痕也不是我弄的。

我不知道何時開始變成這樣的，但這樣的情況切切實實地發生了，並且是到處也在發生。如果你不相信我，你可以自行去查證。很簡單，你只需要鏟子和時間，那就足夠了。

不過我們可能時間無多了。如果你不明白我為何這樣說，那是因為你還未問自己，為甚麼我要這樣做。

你想想，如果那些死去的人寧願往下爬，爬向地獄的話，那麼那些從我們上方襲來、更可怕的東西會是甚麼？

The Cure for Cancer

In a miraculous breakthrough for modern science, we have finally come up with a way to destroy the tissues that make up cancer!

Bloodstains, thick and fresh, led out of the kitchen. A crimson breadcrumb trail ran up the stairs, towards the bedrooms, while downstairs the radio was still blaring.

It appears that the cells respond to a certain frequency of sound, whereby they will just self–destruct. Investigations and tests have been carried out to determine if there are any adverse side–effects, but thus far there have been none: the patient simply disposes of the cells as fecal matter.

On the door handle, a convoluted pattern of red. Fresh blood dripped off the knob and onto the floor.

We will be broadcasting this frequency for the next month for anyone who happens to be a cancer victim. If you know anybody who has cancer, please get them to tune in to the television from 19:00 to 21:00, or simply download the tune from our website and listen to it for twenty minutes!

A carpet soaked with blood,

This is the second day of broadcasting.

癌症治療

這簡直是現代科學的奇蹟突破，我們終於有方法可以破壞製造癌細胞的組織了！

廚房裏鋪著一條新鮮而濃厚的血路，染成深紅色的麵包碎屑形成了另一條小路，沿著樓梯延伸至睡房方向，只剩收音機在樓下廣播著。

那些細胞會對某個頻率的聲音有反應，然後就會自我摧毀。專家經過多重調查及測試後，表示相關療法並無任何有害副作用，那些細胞只會像一般排泄物般被病人排出體外。

門把印有複雜的紅色圖案，鮮血滴在地上 。

接下來的一個月我們都會在此頻道為癌症患者進行廣播。如果你認識一些癌症患者，請呼籲他們於晚上七點至九點期間收看電視，或到我們的網站下載播放器後，即可免費收聽二十分鐘的廣播！

那張染血地氈的旁邊，

今天是第二天的廣播。

On the floor, a knife as sharp as heartbreak, dripping.

Thank you for listening.

A young mother, wrists cut and bloody, lying on the floor by her bed. A picture frame on the bedside depicts a happy family of three with the dad's picture cut out. Coins and notes littered the floor, a sum total of assets that were never meant to be spent.

God be blessed.

The broadcasting for the cure plays, but its tune doesn't reach the second floor.

In her frozen arms was her son, his head swollen with a tumor, hugging the pillow that took his life three days ago.

還有一把鋒利的刀，與心碎的她一同淌著血。

感謝您的收聽。

一位年輕母親倒臥在床邊的地上，手腕割開了，鮮血淋漓。床頭掛著一幀一家三口的全家福，唯獨是爸爸的樣子被剪走了。零錢和紙幣散落一地，一切財物如今已成塵土。

感謝主。

有關治療癌症的廣播繼續放送著，但收音機的聲音傳不到去二樓。

僵硬了的她，抱著頭部因腫瘤而脹大了的兒子；而兒子抱著的，是三天前奪走了他性命的枕頭。

I was on a Reality Dating Show

When I was 25, I went on a reality dating show. I was in between jobs at the time and living with my parents. So, when my friend Michelle mentioned (with a wicked grin) that it might be fun to attend a casting call downtown, I figured what the hell.

It turned out they liked me, and after weeks of paperwork and me basically signing my life away for three months, I was in the final sixteen. Before I knew it, I was flying down to L.A. My parents were skeptical, but I assured them I wasn't serious about it. I painted it as a "last hurrah" kind of thing before I settled into responsible adulthood.

I was picked up and driven to a mansion in the hills, and it was *beautiful*. We had our first mixer with Aaron, the guy whose affections we were supposed to be vying for. He seemed OK, but not my type. I was honestly just happy to have a free trip and booze.

We had some pretty obvious alcoholics and too–wild–for–TV types, so I actually managed to squeak through a couple of eliminations. There were things about the show that I hated, though. The shooting hours were ridiculous, and some of us actually got yelled at once for not staying up to party and create content (after a fourteen–hour day).

約會真人秀

二十五歲那年我參加了約會真人秀，那時我跟父母一起住，而且剛好是工作的空檔期，朋友 Michelle 說市中心有個試鏡活動，建議我去試試看。她（奸笑著）說那一定會很好玩，我倒是覺得好玩個屁。

結果那些工作人員挺喜歡我，幾個星期以來一直在跟他們簽文件，基本上就是確認我在那三個月內，要把整個人生交給他們之類的條款。我當時還不知道自己入圍了十六強，我還坐飛機去洛杉磯呢！我父母對這個節目心存懷疑，但我向他們保證我不會太上心。我只是把它當作我正式踏入成人生涯前的一次「最後狂歡」。

工作人員把我接載到一間座落在山上的豪宅，那是一間*非常壯觀*的豪宅。第一個跟我配對的是 Aaron，他有著人見人愛的魅力，人品也不錯，但不是我喜歡的類型。坦白說我只是單純地對於有個免費旅程，又有免費酒可以喝這回事很高興。

參賽者當中有幾個頗明顯的酒鬼，有幾個則是太瘋狂不適宜上電視，所以我在幾次淘汰中也僥倖「生還」。但節目有幾樣東西讓我很討厭，例如他們的拍攝時間很荒謬，有一次我們其中幾個人因為睡了沒有去派對，工作人員就瘋狂罵我們對拍攝製作沒有貢獻（但那天已經拍了十四個小時）。

That stuff sucked, but I didn't really want to leave until Amanda's elimination. I had two weird discoveries that left me unsettled. The first was that when I woke up the next morning and Amanda's luggage was still there. The crew looked embarrassed when I asked about it, and they whisked it away quickly.

The second thing came later, when Jennifer threw a Frisbee down the hill at the end of the property, and I went looking for it. Hidden behind some tall grass were three freshly dug plots of land. I immediately felt sick to my stomach.

I exaggerated my stomach pains and begged to be taken to the hospital, and once we were there, I told the producer I didn't want to return to the show. Maybe I imagined it, but I thought I saw cold fury flicker across her face. She calmly tried to reason with me, but I held firm. My spidey senses were tingling. I wanted to go home.

Michelle thought I was insane when I told her why I left. But one morning, I got an email from her that just included a link to a news article and read: "WTFFFFFFF."

The cover picture was the mansion I'd stayed in. The headline, "15 Bodies Found at Bel Air Estate."

雖然很討厭，但我還是不想離開這裏，直到 Amanda 被淘汰後，我才察覺不妥。有兩件事讓我很忐忑不安，第一件事是在 Amanda 被淘汰後那天，我起床時還看到她的行李。我向工作人員問起這回事時，他們都顯得很窘迫，然後匆匆忙忙地把她的行李拿走了。

之後再發生了第二件事。那時我跟 Jennifer 在玩拋接飛盤，她把飛盤拋到了豪宅的後面，跌到了山坡下面，然後我就走過去把它撿回來。我看見了地下有三個剛剛挖好的洞，隱藏在一些長得很高的草叢後面。我的胃隨即翻滾起來。

我故意把我的病情説得很嚴重，哀求工作人員讓我到醫院檢查。當我到達醫院之後，我跟製作人説我不想再回去拍攝了。可能是我多心了，但我總覺得她臉上好像閃過了一下怒意。她平靜地嘗試説服我留下來，但我去意已決，因為我的第六感「危險信號」已經在叮叮作響了。我要回家。

當我告訴 Michelle 我離開的原因時，她以為我瘋了。但有天早上我收到她的電郵，裏面是一篇新聞報導的連結，她寫著：「他媽媽媽媽的甚麼鬼東西⋯⋯」

新聞報導的封面照就是我之前住的那間豪宅，標題寫道：「Bel Air 莊園發現十五具屍體」。

Little Bastard

Every year I ask my 2nd graders to draw a picture of whatever scares them most. We discuss the drawings in class. It helps the kids confront their fears and control them.

Sharks in the 70s. Clowns and nuclear bombs in the 80s. Serial killers in the 90s. Lately, guns and lockdowns. Some fears are silly, and others I can't even bear to talk about. But since the beginning, one subject has appeared with astonishing regularity, two or three in every class.

Aside from slight variations in perspective and style, it's always basically the same picture. A boy sits high in the trees that grow on the grounds of the middle school next door, on the opposite side of our playground fence. He's flinging rocks at terrified children below.

"God help the little bastard I catch throwing rocks," we teachers would say to each other.

But we never caught anyone. Middle schoolers are quicker than minnows. And the victims were no help, refusing to tattle or return fire. My colleagues believed it was a perverse rite of passage: smaller children endured the abuse until it was their turn to throw rocks at future generations.

混蛋小孩

我每年都會叫班上的二年級學生畫一幅畫，題目是「最害怕的東西」。我們會在課堂上討論他們的畫作，這樣有助他們面對及控制自己的恐懼。

七十年代的孩子害怕鯊魚；小丑和核彈是八十年代孩子們最怕的東西；九十年代就變成了連環殺人犯；最近則是槍械和禁錮。他們有些恐懼很可笑，其他的更加不值一提。但有一樣東西，從一開始便不斷重複出現，每班都會有兩三位學生畫「他」，非常奇怪。

除了角度和風格有些微差異之外，他們畫的基本上都是同一個畫面：在我校遊樂場欄柵對面，有個小男孩坐在隔壁中學的樹上，樹下站了幾個孩子，那個小男孩用石頭丟向他們，把他們嚇壞了。

「那個丟石頭的小混蛋死定了！」老師們之間會這樣說著。

但那些中學生眨眼就長大了，我們還是抓不到任何人。而那些受害者既不肯透露有關欺凌的事，又不願意反擊。同事們認為那是一個惡性循環：年紀比較小的孩子受到欺凌卻默默忍受著，到他們長大了，就換他們來用石頭丟其他年紀小的孩子。

In class each year, I'd hold up an assortment of the perennial drawings.

"What are these about?" I'd ask. "Bullies?"

The kids would shake their heads.

"Ghosts," they'd say.

Here's the weirdest part. They always drew that boy the same way. Red hat, one eye slightly bigger than the other, brown shoes. How was I supposed to explain that? I couldn't. All I could do was give those poor kids my speech about bullies, and stuff their drawings into my desk drawer with the rest of them.

Then last summer, the middle school chopped down the trees and built a new gymnasium in their place. All the teachers were thrilled.

"No more rocks," we said to each other.

No more ghosts, I thought.

So imagine my surprise when more than half my class drew that damn picture again this year. Sure, the trees were

隨後每年我還是會重複收到不少有關那個男孩的畫作。

「這是關於甚麼的？」我問道：「欺凌嗎？」

孩子們都會搖搖頭。

「鬼怪。」他們回答。

來到最奇怪的地方了，那些學生對那個男孩的描畫每次都是一樣的。他戴著紅色帽子，有一隻眼比另一隻眼大一點，穿著啡色鞋子。我解釋不了這個現象，只好向那些可憐的孩子們說道理，教他們欺凌是件壞事，然後把他們的畫作連同其他描畫男孩的畫作一同收進我的抽屜裏。

直到上年夏天，隔壁中學把樹砍掉了，然後在那個位置建了一間新的體育館。我和其他老師們全都欣喜若狂。

「再沒有石頭了！」老師們都這樣說。

*再沒有鬼怪了！*我心想。

但我今年再次收到那張該死的畫作，這次甚至有半班學生也畫了這樣的畫。你能想像我有多驚訝嗎？那些樹確實被體育

replaced by the gymnasium and the ghost boy was gone, but the rest was the same—children crying, bleeding, flinching, crouching in the dirt.

I spread out the drawings on my desk and called up Tanner, a kid I trust to be a straight-shooter.

"What is this?" I asked. "The boy's gone. He can't throw rocks at you anymore."

"Not at us," said Tanner, pointing at something in each picture. I dug out the drawings from previous years and Tanner went on pointing at those too. "He was aiming at her."

A little girl. Lemon yellow dress. Hair in pigtails. I hadn't noticed her before because she'd been cowering with the other children, afraid.

Not anymore. In the newest drawings she was standing tall, chin up. Smiling.

Tanner spoke in a whisper, almost too soft to hear.
"And now there's nobody to stop her."

館取替了，而那個鬼男孩也確實不見了，可是，畫作中其他的東西還在⋯⋯那些孩子在哭鬧著、流著血，在泥地裏迴避蜷縮著。

我把那些畫作攤在桌面，然後叫了 Tanner 過來，他是個坦白正直的孩子，我很信任他。

「你知道這是甚麼嗎？」我問道：「男孩不見了，他不會再向你丟石頭了。」
「不是丟我們啊，」Tanner 邊在每張畫上指著一些東西，邊回答說。我把之前存下來的畫作全部拿出來，Tanner 也在那些畫上指著。「他是在丟她。」

一個穿著檸檬黃色裙子、紮著辮子的小女孩。她跟其他嚇壞了的孩子蜷縮在一起，所以我之前一直沒有注意到她。

但她現在不再是個嚇壞了的孩子，在最新的畫作裏面，她趾高氣揚的站著，臉上掛著笑容。

Tanner 以氣聲說著，我幾乎聽不見他說甚麼：
「現在沒有人阻止她了。」

Meeting Death

The first thing Death said to me was: "I'm sorry."

His voice was like an old man that had outlived his children, and when I heard it, all the courage that I had built up since I had gotten the call from the doctor drained out of me. I fell to my knees and started crying.

"Why me?" I blubbered as Death walked towards me.

He was a large man, but the shadowy cloak he dragged across the floor was even larger.

I was sniveling now. "I just graduated, I was going to backpack across Europe, I was gonna... I was gonna... Why does it have to be me?"
"It had to be someone," Death answered. "And it turned out to be you."

Eventually, I calmed down.

"Damn it, I promised myself I would put on a brave face when it was time to... time to go. But I guess everyone breaks down when it's their time, right?" I say.
"I don't... remember," Death says.

"What do you mean?"

遇見死神

死神跟我説的第一句話是「對不起」。

他説話時像白頭人送黑頭人的老伯般，語帶遺憾。本來我因為接到醫生的電話而充滿正能量，但我聽到死神那句話後，所有勇氣都徹底消失了。我跪在地上抱頭痛哭。

「為甚麼是我？」死神向我走過來，我放聲大哭。

他身形很高大，但他身上那長得拖地的黑袍更是巨大。

我抽泣著説：「我才剛剛畢業，還打算做個背包客遊歷歐洲……我還想……還想……為甚麼會是我？」
「總要有人充當這個角色的吧，」死神回答：「只是今次選中你而已。」

最後我還是冷靜了下來。

「該死的！我跟自己説過大限將至的時候，我要一臉自豪的，但我想每個人來到這個時候都會崩潰吧，對嗎？」我問道。
「我……想不起來。」死神回答。

「這話是甚麼意思？」

"I know that I've visited countless people, but I can't remember any of them. I think I was like you once, a long time ago; before cities, before governments. As the years passed, my memory began slipping away."

"Wait, are you saying that you used to be human?"
"I am human."

"Well then, after all this time, how are you still alive?"
"I wouldn't describe my existence as truly living. My memory wasn't the only thing to fail with time. My sight became cloudy, my skin became cracked and rough, my bones began to creak and ache, and sometimes I fear I'm losing my mind."

He turns, and even though I can't make out the face beyond the hood of his cloak, I can feel him staring intently at me.

"But some things remain, like my hunger and my thirst; two things that, no matter what I do, I can't seem to sate."

I'm not sure what he means but I steel myself for what comes next anyway. "Do what you need to do. I'm not afraid to die."

「我記得我曾經拜訪過無數的人，但我對他們一點印象也沒有。我想我很久以前應該像你一樣吧，真的很久了，那時沒有城市，也沒有政府⋯⋯隨著歲月流逝，我的記憶也逐漸消褪了。」

「等一下，你是說，你曾經也是人類？」
「我現在也是人類啊。」

「那麼，過了這麼長時間，為甚麼你還活著？」
「我不會用『活著』來形容我的存在。我不只記憶逐漸消褪，還有視覺變得模糊、皮膚變得粗糙乾裂、關節開始僵硬並酸痛起來，有些時候又很怕自己會發瘋。」

他轉身了，雖然他袍上的兜帽遮住了他的臉，我看不見他的樣子，但我感覺到他正凝視著我。

「但也有些感覺沒有消褪，例如飢餓感和飢渴感，無論我做甚麼也好，始終沒法滿足這兩種感覺。」

雖然不太明白他說甚麼，但我把心一橫，無論之後會發生甚麼事，我也無所畏懼了。「要殺要剁，悉隨尊便，我不怕死！」

"Neither am I." Death says, and with that, he turns away from me and throws off his cloak.

As I take in his form, I gasp and stagger back. His skin is pale and flakey, he is stick–thin; his arms and legs are like fleshy rods and his ribs are almost sticking out of his chest. And then, as if he were made of dust, he's blown away.

Later, as I'm tearing through my fridge, I vaguely notice that Death's cloak is still on the floor. After I empty my fridge of all the water, soda and beer in it, I head downstairs to the basement where I keep my emergency water. I tear open the plastic packaging and chug all the water bottles I have stored.

But nothing helps. I'm still so thirsty.

「我也不怕。」死神回答，説罷就轉身背對著我，把袍子扔掉。

當我看到他的真面目後，我不禁倒抽了一口涼氣，跟蹌地向後退。他皮膚很蒼白，而且嚴重脱皮，手腳瘦得像幾根筷子般，活像個火柴人，肋骨也像快要撐破皮膚了。然後他就如塵土般，隨風飄散了。

回過神來，我已在冰箱前哭成淚人，矓曨間注意到死神的袍子還在地上。我把冰箱裏的水、汽水和啤酒全部一飲而盡後，再跑到地下室找緊急用水。我把那些塑膠製的包裝統統撕開，把所有儲備的樽裝水都倒進嘴裏。

可是全都沒用，我還是很口渴。

Sympathy Pains

When my girlfriend first announced that we were expecting, I was overjoyed. My own father hadn't been around for my childhood, so I wanted to make sure that things would be different for my kid. Stepping up to the plate and becoming the best father I could be was the only option. Just because Felicia was the one carrying our child, I wasn't going to be any less a part of this journey.

Each day into the pregnancy, Felicia and I grew more synchronised. When she had morning sickness, I was nauseous too. When her bladder ached, so did mine. When she felt the baby kicking, my insides received a nudge. "Sympathy pains" was what my mother called it. She told me that men get them all the time and found the whole situation amusing. My friends reacted similarly, poking fun at how postmodern I was acting. No one truly understood. The cramps, the heartburn, the swelling– it was all beginning to feel too real.

Over the months, my physical state deteriorated, eventually overshadowing that of my pregnant partner. While I confined myself to the house, Felicia continued with life as normal. Embarrassed and emasculated, all I could do in my feeble condition was depend on her. By the time of our baby shower, my "sympathy pains" had become unimaginable. Having finally coaxed me out of the house, my loved ones

擬娩症候群

我們一直很期待新生命的到來，所以當女朋友跟我說「你要當爸爸了」的時候，我簡直是欣喜若狂！自童年起，我父親就很少在我身邊，所以我想確保自己的子女不會有這樣的童年。我唯一能做的，就是要從現在開始，努力做個最好的父親。既然 Felicia 已經替我懷了孩子，我就更加不能錯過這趟懷孕旅程的每一個細節！

懷孕期一天一天過去，我和 Felicia 變得愈來愈同步，例如在她晨吐時，我也會有噁心的感覺；在她膀胱酸痛時，我的膀胱也會跟著酸痛起來；當寶寶踢她肚子時，我也會覺得好像有東西在肚子裏面推了一下。我媽媽說這是「擬娩症候群」，她還說準爸爸們通常都會有這個症狀，還覺得整個狀況很有趣。我的朋友也覺得很有趣，還嘲弄著我的反應很「後現代」。但沒有人真的懂我，那些絞痛、胃部的灼熱感，還有水腫，這一切都開始讓我覺得過分真實了。

過去幾個月以來，我的身體狀況愈來愈差，比懷孕的女朋友還要差。情況變成了是我足不出戶，而 Felicia 卻繼續正常生活，沒有異樣。雖然這樣使我很難堪，而且男子氣概盡失，但我虛弱得只能依靠她照顧我。到了臨產前一個月舉辦的迎嬰派對，我的擬娩症使我折騰得要命。親友們終於成功勸誘我走出屋外，但他們馬上就後悔了。

immediately wished they hadn't.

Pale, emaciated and bearing a distended abdomen, I'm now a ghost of myself. Whatever it is I'm suffering, I know I can't survive it for much longer.

Right as we're opening the presents is when my stomach finally gives way, splitting down the middle like a piñata. Blood and intestines pour from my midsection. Amidst the chaos, Felicia drops to my side and soothes me as if she were a trained midwife. Lifting her sundress, she peels back a layer of prosthetic skin, revealing a cushion where our 9–month fetus should be. I don't even have the strength to be angry.

"B–but you said we were pregnant…"
"We are pregnant, darling" she chirps back, unfazed.

"W–what's happening to me? Is this…s–sympathy pains?" I croak deliriously. Consciousness fading, I can glimpse a small figure stirring to life in my entrails.
"Oh, Michael" laughs Felicia, her smile more alien to me than ever. "I know you humans prefer the term 'sympathy pains'. But on my planet, when a male gives birth, we just call it labour."

腹脹如鼓的我，既蒼白又憔悴，好像沒有靈魂似的。我不知
道正折騰我的是甚麼，我只知道我快熬不住了。

正當大家興高采烈地拆禮物的時候，我突然像個皮納塔娃娃
般，腹部位置攔腰裂開了，鮮血和腸子滾滾湧出來。在一片
混亂之中，Felicia 走過來跪在我旁邊，像個受過專業訓練的
助產士般安撫我。然後她掀起了她的背心裙，把一層假體皮
膚撕下來後，展露著一個靠墊，她的肚子竟然不是我們那九
個月大的胎兒！？但我已經沒有多餘的力氣動怒了。

「但……但你不是說我要當爸爸了嗎……？」
「沒錯啊親愛的，你是要當爸爸了啊。」她輕快地回答，非
常鎮定。

「那……那我是怎麼了？這不是擬……擬娩症候群嗎？」我
口齒不清、聲音沙啞地說著。隨著意識逐漸模糊，我瞥見了
有個細小的人影在我五臟六腑裏蠕動著。
「噢對了，Michael，」Felicia 哈哈地說，她的笑容陌生得
像個外星人。「你們人類喜歡用『擬娩症候群』這個詞語嘛，
但在我的星球，當雄性產子的時候，我們還是稱之為『分
娩』。」

All Watered Down

Since the coma, I've barely been able to handle my visits with Karen. It feels like I'm talking to a shell, one that can't hear my repeated apologies. The last time we spoke, Karen had begged me to get her out. "Please, Cheryl! I'm normal now! The tide is out – please take me with you. All this water under my skin got me feeling all washed out. You gotta get me outta here!"

I looked into frantic eyes, brushed her tangled hair from her face and said, "No, baby. I can't take you until you're better."

She slammed her fists on her legs, "I'm gonna be nothing but water inside! **HE'LL HAVE ME DROWNING! HE'S GONNA DROWN ME!**" The nurses wrestled her away as she screamed that she hated me. That night, she beat her head against a wall in her room. She hasn't woken up since.

So, everyday after work I stop by for as long as I can stand to beg forgiveness from the husk of the woman I loved. Without the staff here, I don't know if I could take it. The nurses are so kind, and really seem to care about us. While I'm not religious, I can still appreciate their kind words of consolation and their repeated prayers for Karen. This small facility came highly recommended to us, and seeing as it was just outside of Fort Worth, it seemed perfect.

全都稀釋掉

自從 Karen 昏迷之後，探望她成了一件令我難過的事。那種感覺就像跟一個空洞的軀殼講話般，她聽不見我不斷的道歉。我們最後一次對話時，Karen 哀求我帶她離開這裏。「Cheryl，我求求你！我現在已經正常了！已經潮退了，拜託你帶我走……我體內的那些水會把我的感覺全都洗掉……你一定要帶我離開這裏！」

我望著她幾近發狂的眼神，我梳理著她打結的頭髮，並說：「不可以的，親愛的，待你好轉了我才帶你走。」

她猛然地用拳頭搥了自己的腿，「我整個人都會變成水！**他會把我淹死！他想淹死我！**」她尖叫著說很討厭我，幾個護士立即把她制服。就在當晚，她在房間裏將頭撞向牆壁，然後就一直沒有醒過來。

我每天下班都會去看一看她，我竭盡所能只為了讓我愛的女人原諒自己。沒有醫護人員的陪同，我不知道自己能否應付得來。護士都很和藹可親，似乎真的很關心我們。雖然我沒有宗教信仰，但我很感激他們的慰問，也很感激他們為 Karen 祈禱。這座小小的設施很有名氣，而且它位於沃思堡市外不遠處，非常方便。

Tonight, I fall asleep holding Karen's hand. I wake up with a start, glance at my watch. It's 10:30 – well after visiting hours. Did the nurses forget I was here? I shuffle around in the dark room, lit only by the light coming from the window to the hallway. I sit back down as my vision adjusts to the darkness. Glancing up, I am suddenly staring into Karen's eyes, the whites so big they're almost glowing. I jump back, knocking over my chair and cursing.

"Jesus Christ! Karen, are you awake?"

Her eyes somehow grow wider and her clenched jaw opens just enough to hiss, "You can't still be here! He's gonna water you down..."

"What? Karen, what are you talking ab –"

The door behind me creaks open, and one of Karen's doctors stands in the lit doorway.

"Why, Ms Cheryl. What are you doing here?" He pulls a full hypodermic needle from his scrub pocket, and readies the plunger, squirting out a tiny bit of the clear fluid inside. "It's well past visiting hours."

As he steps forward I realize how large he is and I freeze.

這晚，我牽著 Karen 的手睡著了。我抖了一下，驚醒了。我望一望錶，已經是十點半了，探病時段已經過了很久。難道那些護士忘記了我在這裏嗎？我單靠連接著走廊的窗戶透進來的微弱燈光，在黑沉沉的房間裏到處走著。當我的眼睛適應了黑暗的環境後，我回到本來的位置坐下。我抬頭望向 Karen 的雙眼，她的眼白範圍很大，幾近發光。我嚇得跳了起來，碰跌了椅子，還嚇得飆了髒話。

「我的天啊！Karen，你醒了嗎？」

她眼睛莫名其妙地愈睜愈大，原本緊咬著的雙唇也微微張開了，低聲地說：「不要在這裏逗留！他會把你稀釋……」

「甚麼？Karen，你在說甚……」

我身後的門吱聲地打開了，其中一個負責看顧 Karen 的醫生站在有光的走廊上。

「咦，Cheryl 小姐，你在這裏幹嘛呢？」他從醫生袍的口袋裏拿出一枝針筒，按下了活塞，把裏面透明的液體擠了一點出來。「探病時段已經過了很久了喔。」

他向我走近時，我才發現他有多龐大，我完全愣住了。

"Don't worry, honey," he says, leaning in to whisper in my ear, "We'll fix you right up. By the time I'm done with y'all, you'll be normal women."

I feel a prick in my arm as I finally think to scream, but his hand is already over my mouth.

The last thing I hear before the world turns to a haze is Karen's quiet, strained voice, "He's gonna water us down until we're nothing."

「寶貝，不用害怕。」他靠近我耳邊低聲跟我說：「我們馬上就會治好你，當我把你們都治好了，你們便會是正常的女人了。」

正當我意識到要尖叫時，手臂就傳來一陣刺痛感，他還用手掩著我的嘴巴，讓我吭不出聲。

我在世界變得混沌前聽到的最後一句話，是 Karen 平靜又氣若柔絲的聲音說道：「他會把我們稀釋掉，直到我們甚麼也不是……」

Desert Roads

Our road–trip is always something special. Picking up Eddie marked the beginning of the annual adventure.

He didn't look himself as he walked out of his house, a hoodie pulled tight and tinted glasses were not usual Eddie.

"I'm sick," he replied in a hoarse voice, avoiding eye contact, "I'll just sleep on the way there."

He threw his usual suitcase in the trunk, but along with that a much larger duffel bag that looked strangely heavy. Weird, but oh well; we were finally en route, destination: Vegas.

Three hours into driving we finally hit the desert roads. Eddie was uncharacteristically un–talkative, and his face was as pale as a sheet, but when I asked if he was feeling alright, he responded with nothing more than a dismissive shrug. I was expecting a long–winded tangent about feeling fine, so I assumed he really was quite ill.

The first real sign of something odd was when I heard the noise. It wasn't much, but after driving for five hours on the empty, desert roads, any sound sticks out. It was just a small bump from the back of the car, nothing too weird. What really chilled me was what followed, I swear I heard a whisper of the word "Help" come from the back. Eddie denied he

沙漠公路

我們每次旅程都總是充滿著驚喜,而這趟年度歷險的首要任務,就是去接載 Eddie。

Eddie 從家中走出來,穿著連帽衞衣的他,把兜帽的繩子綁得很緊,還戴著一副有色眼鏡,跟平時的他很不一樣,我幾乎看不出來是他。

「我生病了,」他回答時聲音很沙啞,又迴避我的眼神,「我在車上睡一下就好了。」

Eddie 把他常用的那個行李箱,還有一個看起來異常重的巨型行李袋一同丟進車尾廂。唔,有點奇怪⋯⋯不過我們總算踏上了旅途,向拉斯維加斯出發!

過了三小時,車子終於駛到了沙漠公路。Eddie 一反常態地安靜,面色更是蒼白如紙。我問他有沒有事,他卻只不屑地聳了聳肩,沒有作聲。我本以為他會説一大堆無關痛癢的廢話,來表達自己還好,但看他這樣的反應,我想他真的是病得很重吧。

但當我聽見有些聲響時,我才愈覺得不妥。那聲音雖然很微弱,但我在這空曠的沙漠公路上駕了五小時的車,現在就算再微小的聲音我也能聽得一清二楚。本來只是車廂後傳來小

heard anything and went back to sleep, but I could almost sense he was faking the slumber.

Finally pulling into a gas station, he stirred a bit and rubbed his face, to both our surprises his hand came back with blood on it. He mumbled something about a nosebleed and ran to the bathroom.

I tried to not think too much of it, but as I stood pumping gas in the muggy night air, something caught my attention, the same bump that I heard earlier, coming distinctly from my own car's trunk. A mix of fear and intrigue got the best of me, and I slowly pried open the hatch.

My heart skipped a beat when I saw his duffle bag move. It looked like he wasn't coming out of the bathroom anytime soon, and my curiosity was killing me, so I had to look inside.

A wretched stench hit me as I unzipped the long bag, but the inside contents were more nauseating than any odor.

Looking back at me was Eddie, missing the entirety of the skin from his neck upwards. With what sounded like his last breath, he warned me with one word. "**Run**".

小的「碰」一聲，沒甚麼大不了。真正嚇倒我的是隨後的聲音，我發誓聽到了從車廂後面傳出來、很小聲的「救命」。Eddie 堅持說他甚麼也聽不到，然後又睡著了。我開始懷疑他其實是在裝睡……

車子終於駛到了油站，Eddie 驚醒了，然後揉了揉自己的臉。手放下來之後，我倆都嚇呆了，因為他雙手全都是血。他呢喃著甚麼流鼻血之類的話後，就衝到了洗手間。

我盡量不去胡思亂想，但當我在這個悶熱侷促的晚上，呆滯地替車子入著油的時候，又聽見了之前的「碰」一聲，我直覺認為那是從我車子的車尾廂裏傳出的。我既驚慌又好奇，最後還是把這個像潘朵拉盒子般神秘的車尾廂緩緩打開了。

我看見 Eddie 的行李袋在動！嚇得我心臟也幾乎跳了出來。但看來他不會那麼快從洗手間回來，而我的好奇心已經爆發了，於是我決定要一探究竟。

甫拉開袋子的拉鏈，一股惡臭馬上襲來。不過，裏面的東西比那股氣味更加令人作嘔。

在袋裏的 Eddie 跟我對望，但他頸以上的皮膚全都不見了。奄奄一息的他吐出最後一句話來警告我：「**快跑**……」

Julia was a Very Bad Girl

Julia waited patiently for her father. He had promised to stop by on his way home from work to pick her up something to eat. Today was a Thursday though, and Julia knew her father stayed late to catch up on work on Thursdays. So she waited.

After a while, Julia began to worry. It seemed like daddy was taking longer than usual. Of course, she didn't have a clock in her room, and daddy had boarded up all the windows, so she had no way of knowing for sure. Julia tried to calm down, but her eleven year old mind was going through all the terrible things that might have befallen her father.

As more time passed, Julia wondered if her father was staying away on purpose, as punishment for her screaming at him the other day. If it was a punishment, then Julia knew she deserved it. It was how it had always been.

Months ago, when daddy had woken her up in the middle of the night, touching her in weird ways, and telling her how much she looked like her long gone mother, Julia had attacked him in a fit of rage. She tried to make it up to him the next day, but all daddy said was that he finally saw her for the unholy temptress that she was and punished her for being bad by shackling her to her bed. He had boarded up the windows after the nice mailman had seen her through one and had tried to break into the house. Daddy had killed him in front of Julia to show her the consequences of her actions.

壞女孩 Julia

Julia 耐心等待著爸爸回家，因為他答應了 Julia 回家時會買東西給她吃。但今天是星期四，Julia 知道爸爸逢星期四都要追趕工作進度，會晚一點才能回家，所以她乖乖等著。

過了一會兒，Julia 開始有點擔心了，爸爸還沒回家，而且好像比平時更遲了。但由於她房間沒有時鐘，窗戶又被爸爸用木板封了起來，所以她根本無法得知實際時間。Julia 嘗試保持冷靜，但只有十一歲的她，不禁胡亂猜想著爸爸是否遭遇到甚麼不測，腦海裏上映著一幕幕驚心動魄的假設場面。

時間一分一秒地流逝，Julia 在想是否因為她之前在爸爸面前大吵大鬧，所以他故意不回家來懲罰自己。如果爸爸真的要這樣懲罰自己，Julia 知道這也是她應得的教訓。況且爸爸每次也是這樣懲罰自己的。

幾個月前有一晚，爸爸突然半夜叫醒了 Julia，雙手不安分的觸碰著她，並告訴她長得有多像早已離去的媽媽。Julia 一怒之下就動手打了他。到了第二天，Julia 嘗試與爸爸和好，但爸爸堅持說她本就是個墮落、勾引男人的妖婦，現在終於露出狐狸尾巴。於是爸爸就把 Julia 綁在床上，作為她使壞的懲罰。有一次，有位好心的郵差先生在屋外看到了被綁的 Julia，試著闖進她家。那次之後，爸爸就把所有窗戶

Julia pressed her face into her sheets and started to cry, as her hunger and the memories of her past sins overwhelmed her. If only her father were here, she would apologize to him and promise not to seduce men anymore.

Her ears perked up as she heard the front door open. She lifted her head up and wiped her tears as she heard heavy footsteps sound throughout the house. Might it be— But no. As the door to her room swung open, she took in the sight of two tall men, dressed in dark blue uniforms. They looked like the kind of people daddy had told her to avoid, but as she looked at the two males, Julia felt her previous teary eyed resolutions fade.

She slowly lifted her blood stained sundress over her head and beckoned to the two strangers. The closest one, who was talking frantically into a radio, suddenly stopped and walked over to her with a glazed look in his eyes. As he caressed her, Julia pulled his face close to hers and started running her jagged teeth against the strange man's neck. As she bit down, Julia knew she was being a bad girl and that daddy wouldn't approve.

But she couldn't help it, she thought, as his lifeblood flowed into her open mouth, she was so hungry.

都用木板封了起來。爸爸還在 Julia 面前把那個郵差殺了，以收殺雞儆猴之效。

在飢餓感和回想起過去罪孽的折磨下，Julia 把臉埋在被子裏，哭了起來。她邊哭邊想，如果爸爸回來的話，她一定會向他道歉，而且會答應他以後不再勾引男人。

Julia 聽見有人打開了前門，精神馬上振作起來。之後屋裏傳來沉重的腳步聲，她抬起頭，擦乾眼淚，心裏想道：可能是……？非也。Julia 的房門打開了，兩個穿著深藍色制服的高大男人出現在眼前。他們看起來像是爸爸叫她要小心的那種人，但當她望著那兩個男人時，本來哭得模糊的視野逐漸變得清晰。

Julia 緩緩地把自己那染血的背心裙掀起蓋過頭，然後向那兩個陌生人招手。靠近 Julia 的那位先生，本來正喋喋不休地向著對講機說話，他突然停了下來，目光呆滯的走近 Julia。當那位先生伸手輕撫 Julia 之際，她把臉龐貼近他的臉龐，然後用鋸齒狀的牙齒狠狠噬進這個陌生男人的脖子裏。當 Julia 一口咬下去的時候，她深知自己很壞，爸爸肯定會非常不滿。

但她實在按捺不住了，本能驅使她張開那血盆大口，吞噬著他的生命，因為她實在太餓了。

Please Ignore My Suicide

Please, please, please, I think desperately to the commuters around me as the train approaches. Please ignore what I'm about to do.

It doesn't seem like anyone is going to intervene this time. The station is usually near empty at this hour and, thankfully, tonight is no exception.

Of course, I understand why people feel the need to play hero and rush to my rescue. But they're wrong. If only they knew how much unnecessary pain and suffering could be prevented by just letting me jump.

I should have died in that damn war. Nothing has ever been the same ever since I was shipped overseas to be screwed up beyond repair. They say that becoming a soldier changes you– but I never expected it to ruin me. I once believed in the power of the common man to help others. But after watching my friends die in front of me, being forced to kill absolute innocents, I no longer see anything in life worth fighting for. My only hope now is for a clean death.

All that's left to do is take my place next to the tracks and make the leap, and I'll finally be free of this miserable existence. As the train draws near, I teeter at the edge of the platform, readying myself to make the final vault forwards.

請無視我的自殺

「拜託了，你們行行好吧……」當火車駛至時，我希望這個絕望的心聲能傳到那些上班族的耳中。請不要阻止我接下來要做的事。

這次似乎沒有人要干預我了。這個時段的車站多數也是空無一人，幸好今晚也不例外。

其實我能理解人們想要充英雄的心態，所以他們會衝過來救我。但他們錯了，因為他們不知道讓我跳下去之後，原來可以減少許多不必要的痛苦和折磨。

在那場該死的戰爭裏，我早該死掉了。自從啟航出海之後，一切都變了，變得一塌糊塗。有人說當兵會改變人生，但我從沒想過這個改變會是摧毀人生。我曾幾何時也相信過人們互助的力量，但當我親眼目睹好友在自己面前死去、自己被迫濫殺無辜之後，我已生無可戀。我現在只求一死。

我只要走到路軌旁，一躍而下，就能擺脫這個痛苦的身份。火車逐漸靠近，我在月台邊跟跟蹌蹌地走著，為踏出最後一步做好準備。

Slowly, I feel the world around me starting to change– the rattle of train wheels becoming enemy gunfire, the blare of the of train horn becoming dying screams.

This is it. Goodbye cruel world.

Out of nowhere, a pair of hands close around my chest, dragging me away from the speeding train. Together, me and the intervening figure tumble backwards.

"Are you alright?!" asks the old man worriedly, his clothing now bearing the camouflage of an enemy uniform.

The last thing I see before I black out is my hands closing around his throat.

By the time I come to, the station is empty. With a sigh, I drag what remains of the man's body into the alley behind the station. Removing a nearby manhole cover, I let his body slide into the sewer with a thump, landing atop a pile of a dozen civilian corpses. A single tear rolls across my face as I gaze down at those poor souls.

Oh God, how I wish. How I wish that people would just let me die...so I could let them live.

我彷彿感覺到周遭的事物正逐漸改變著：火車行駛時發出的轟隆聲變成了敵人的炮火聲，刺耳的喇叭聲變成了垂死的尖叫聲⋯⋯

該完結了，殘酷的世界，再見了。

突然間，有一對手抱著我，把我拉走，遠離高速駛至的火車。然後我和那個莫名出現的人一同往後倒下。

「你還好吧？」一個老伯伯憂心地問道，他身上的衣服在我眼中變成了敵軍的迷彩服。

在我昏過去之前，我看見最後的畫面是我掐著他的脖子。

當我醒過來的時候，車站空無一人。我嘆了一口氣，然後把那個男人破碎的屍體拖到車站的後巷。把附近一個沙井蓋掀開後，我把他的屍體推下去，讓他滑到下水道裏，伏在那些平民的屍體堆上，發出一聲悶響。我向下凝望著那些可憐的百姓，不禁流下了一滴眼淚。

天啊，我衷心希望，希望那些人可以讓我死去⋯⋯這樣他們就可以活下去了。

Erotomania

Jack didn't hold out much hope when he bought the love potion from that strange, old gypsy woman in Little Italy. He thought it was probably a hoax, like fortune telling and crystal balls and all that garbage they peddled to the unwashed masses. If Jack had to be honest, he wouldn't even have given this a second thought if wasn't for the simple fact that he was so lonely.

All his college buddies had dates lined until well after graduation. But Jack was just some scrawny thing, quiet, shy and awkward. For him, it was generally night after lonely night, alone with himself and the laptop watching Netflix. Or maybe just wandering the streets, as he'd been doing when he saw Madam Qurio's shop and entered it on a whim.

He at least wanted a chance, and he was desperate enough to gamble on a surely fake love potion. He listened politely as Madam Qurio told him what it did and gave him the proper instructions on its usage. She was oddly specific about one point: he was to only drink a small bit of it each night – **a drop and no more**. She was very insistent on this one point.

Ignoring her advice, Jack drank it all as soon as he exited the shop, every last drop of the bitter–tasting liquid. He figured if he was going to do it, he might as well do it his way.

情愛妄想症

Jack 在小意大利向一個又老又古怪的吉卜賽女郎買了一瓶「愛情魔藥」，但他對它的功效並沒有抱太大期望。他以為這瓶藥大概跟算命、水晶球或是那些奸商向無知的大眾兜售的垃圾「法寶」一樣，都是騙人的把戲。如果 Jack 不是因為他實在是太過寂寞難耐，他肯定不會二話不說就把那瓶魔藥買下來。

除了他自己之外，大學認識的哥兒們在畢業後，全都馬上有了約會對象。但 Jack 是個瘦弱、安靜、害羞又笨拙的男孩，對他而言，每個晚上都是孤獨荒涼的，獨自一人在家，用手提電腦登入 Netflix 看電影，或者有時會在街上閒逛。那時他就是這樣閒逛著，然後看到 Qurio 女士的商店，心血來潮就走進了店內。

即使他知道這瓶愛情魔藥肯定是假貨，但沮喪的他至少想要一個機會，賭賭看魔藥會不會真的有效。他謙恭地聽著 Quiro 女士說明魔藥的效用和正確使用方法。奇怪的是，她特別指明了一點：每晚只能喝一點點，**一滴就夠了，不能再多**。她特別強調了這項規則。

但 Jack 沒有理會她的建議，他一離開商店就把那瓶藥一飲而盡，把那些苦澀的液體一滴不漏地倒進嘴裏。他覺得既然他要做這件事，就要依自己的方法去做。

That was three days ago. That was where everything went wrong. Terribly wrong.

The potion had worked. Oh, man, had it worked.

Jack was trapped in the basement of his parents' house. He thought no one would find him here, but he was wrong. Somehow, they knew where he was hiding, and were coming for him.

He could hear the sounds of epic battle above him, as the house was turned into a war zone. The weapons going off, metal striking flesh, followed by bodies hitting the ground. Jack thought he could even hear the revving of a chainsaw. There were screams, too:

"Jack! You're the one for me!"
"Jack, dearest, you are my one true love!"
"Jack! Jack! Only I am right for you!"

It was a cacophony of lust and anger, each voice a battle cry, claiming that they were the only ones worthy of Jack's love. The only protection he had left was the heavy basement door. It was sturdy, but they had an unholy amorous furor, attempting to rip the door off its hinges. He knew it wouldn't hold for much longer.

那已經是三天前的事了，也就是一切錯誤的根源，實在錯得太可怕了。

那瓶魔藥奏效了。天啊，它竟然奏效了。

Jack 把自己關在父母家的地下室裏，以為沒有人會找到他。但他錯了，她們不知怎的，竟然得悉他躲在這裏，她們要來找他了。

他聽見像電影般的戰鬥聲從上面傳來，房子好像化身成一個戰爭地帶般。槍枝鏗鏘的開火聲，刀劍切開肉體的聲音，緊接著是身體倒在地上的聲音。Jack 隱約聽到電鋸發動的聲響，也有很多叫喊聲⋯⋯

「Jack！你是我的唯一！」
「我最親愛的 Jack，你是我的真愛！」
「Jack！Jack！只有我才是合適人選！」

那是由色慾和憤怒結合而成的刺耳交響曲，每把吶喊的聲音都在宣稱，她們自己就是唯一值得 Jack 的愛意的真命天女。現在能保護他的只剩那道厚重的地下室門。雖然那扇門很堅固，但她們帶著極端又渴慕的狂熱，企圖把門從鉸鏈上扯下來。他很清楚那扇門熬不了多久。

When the door gave way, they would spill through the narrow doorway and down the stairs, piling on and climbing over each other until they eventually overwhelmed him, drowning him in a sea of desperate, lovesick humanity, each member of the flood only having one goal in mind:

To love him forever. To claim him as their own.

當地下室的門打開了之後，她們會從狹窄的門縫和樓梯裏湧進來，人疊人的爬過來，直至把他浸沒在絕望、病態的苦戀之中。在人潮裏的她們腦海裏只有一個目標：

永遠愛他，並宣稱他是屬於自己的。

Howdy Neighbor Days

My town gets a lot of grief for its annual festival. With a name like "Howdy Neighbor Days" it's fairly easy to see why.

I get it. I really do. It's a goofy, old fashioned name for what I guess is a goofy, old–fashioned idea. For some folks, getting to know your neighbors is hokey.

But in my town, it's essential. We live together in a tight–knit community, and I think that's something worth celebrating, personally.

And, really, the festival isn't very different from any small–town carnival. There are amusement rides, game booths, cotton candy stands, a beer garden. All the normal stuff. I think it's mostly just the name that sets us apart and makes us the subject of ridicule.

If people outside of our town would visit, they'd understand. They'd understand the importance of family, friendship, and community. That's all there is in this life. Those bonds are what give life meaning. Past the nihilism, past the consumerism, of modern life is a simpler way of living.

People in my town get that.

鄰里同樂節

我住的城鎮因為一個年度節日被罵得很慘,它叫做「鄰里同樂節」,原因也很明顯吧。

我懂為甚麼會捱罵,我真的懂。因為它的名字又蠢又老套,所以我猜那應該是個又蠢又老套的活動。對有些人來說,這個活動能讓你知道你的鄰居有多虛偽。

但在我住的城鎮裏,這個節日是不可或缺的。我們住在同一個社區,關係緊密,所以就我而言,這也算是值得慶祝的一回事吧。

但其實我們這個節日跟別人的小鎮嘉年華差不多,一樣有著各式各樣的機動遊戲,也有攤位給大家玩遊戲、吃棉花糖,還有個露天啤酒園,全都是一些正常的東西。我想大概只是它的名字比較與眾不同,使我們成了別人的笑柄。

但如果其他鎮的人也來參加的話,他們就會明白了。這裏會使他們明白到家庭、友誼和社區的重要性,因為我們在這裏生活就是需要這些關係,而這些連結恰好就是我們的生存意義。這裏不提倡虛無主義,也不主張消費主義,我們只是簡簡單單的生活著。

鎮裏的所有人都深深明白這個道理。

Consider how we all come together during the festival. Consider how we're bonded. The things we do make us one. We walk around knowing we're all the same, deep down. Howdy Neighbor Days creates a confederacy of community.

We don't get a lot of strangers to our little festival. We don't advertise it, and besides, you're not a stranger for long when you join in. Sometimes people don't want to join. Sometimes they come to mock and denigrate. That's okay. We take all kinds.

Those people who don't want to join in with the community, well, we've got another purpose for them. They get to be the tie that binds. After all, nothing brings a town together like partaking of the same meal. Just like a church potluck or a block party barbeque, it really engenders community spirit. The anticipation, sitting together smelling the meat roasting over the fire. The conversation around the dinner table. The shared experience of committing the same crime, knowing that they can't turn you in without indicting themselves. That's what builds strong bonds. That's what neighborliness is all about.

There's nothing hokey about that.

試想像在節日期間，我們聚首一堂，陣容多麼鼎盛，關係多麼密切！我們做的事使我們打成一片。我們清楚明白大家的內心都是一樣的，鄰里同樂節使我們的社區團結一致。

這個小小的節日並沒有吸引到很多陌生人過來參與，因為我們沒有對外宣揚是次活動。再者，只要你加入了之後，很快就不再是個陌生人了。有些人不想參與，又有些人過來只是為了嘲笑及貶損我們。但不要緊，任何人我們都很歡迎。

至於那些不想融入社區的人，我們自有另一些活動給他們，他們將成為團結我們鄰里關係的催化劑。畢竟沒有甚麼比一起同享佳餚能使我們更融洽了，就像教堂的團契聚餐，或是在街區派對一起燒烤般，真能在社區裏培養互助互愛的精神呢！一起在火爐邊圍坐著，聞著烤肉的味道；在飯桌一起聊天；分享經驗時發現原來大家都有犯過一樣的罪行，除非把自己的罪行也曝露了，不然他們無法舉報別人。這些就是我們維繫良好關係的方法，這也就是鄰居的意義。

我們一點也不虛偽。

The Twins

Once, there lived a pair of twins who were completely identical from the crown of their head to their toes. The two spoke with the same intonation, the same drops and rises in their speeches, the same soft voice. The people around them always threw the two the same uneasy look, as though uncertain of their own vision. Or maybe they just didn't feel comfortable around them.

Jill and Janet, the two were called. Being identical meant that nobody could really figure out who was who. They shared a mental bond that was so great, they knew when the other was injured.

Like that time when Jill accidentally cut her fingers on the fence, Janet jumped and spilt paint over her canvas, and the tiniest scar appeared on her finger.

Or that time when Janet stepped on a nail, and Jill woke up with a cry, the bottom of her foot blooming a red dot identical to the size of the nail.

It was a curse, they decided, and decided to keep it secret. The townsfolk weren't adverse to burning witches alive. Just the other day, a suspected witch had been drowned in the lake.

雙生兒

從前有一對雙胞胎，她們從頭到腳都長得完全相同。她們說話時有著相同的語調和高低仰揚，連聲音都一模一樣。她們身邊的人通常都會以不安的眼神看著她們，不相信自己的眼睛，以為自己有幻覺。又或者只是他們不喜歡跟她們一起玩而已。

她們倆的名字分別是 Jill 和 Janet，但由於她們長得完全相同，沒有人能真正分得出誰是誰。然而她們的心靈感應很厲害，如果一方受傷了，另一方就會知道。

就像有一次 Jill 不小心被圍欄割傷了手指，Janet 立刻嚇了一跳，打翻了顏料，灑滿了她的畫布。在那之後，Janet 的手指就出現了一道細小的疤痕。

或是有一次 Janet 踩到了一根釘子，Jill 就哭著驚醒過來，後來發現自己腳底長了一個跟釘子一樣大小的紅點。

Jill 和 Janet 認為這是個詛咒，而且決定保守這個秘密。城鎮裏的居民很迷信，會把奇異的女子當成「女巫」，然後把她們活活燒死。就在幾天前，他們將一個懷疑是女巫的女子掉進湖裏，把她淹死。

So when Janet got trampled by a horse–wagon, Jill was out cold for three days. Janet was buried as soon as possible to help Jill to cope with the loss.

When Jill awoke, she was beyond grief. She cried for the whole morning, tearing out chunks of her hair. Her mum found her sitting in Janet's bedroom in a daze, fingernails cracked and bloody, with wounds in her hands that looked like they could have come from wooden splinters.

當 Janet 被馬車輾斃時，Jill 就昏迷了三天。家人很快就把 Janet 埋葬了，希望這樣做會令 Jill 好過一點。

Jill 醒來的時候，她悲痛欲絕，哭了整個早上，又把自己的頭髮一撮一撮地扯下來。她媽媽發現她精神恍惚地坐在 Janet 的睡房裏，她的手指甲全都破掉了，血跡斑斑，而她手上的傷口看來是木刺造成的。

Fun With 911

Operator: 911, what's the address of your emergency?

Caller   : I'm in the walls.

Operator: Sir, I need the address.

Caller   : She doesn't know I'm in the house.

Operator: I need the nature of your emergency. Is anyone in danger?

Caller   : Soon.

Operator: Are you able to tell me what's happening?

Caller   : I've been here for so long. I've been waiting. I will continue to wait.

Operator: Sir, you need to know that playing a joke on 911 is a crime. If this isn't a joke, you need to tell me immediately.

Caller   : No joke. I'm hiding.

Operator: If you cannot say your location, I will need to terminate this call.

Caller   : I'm at 350 Hill Street in Falmouth.

Operator: ...Sir?

Caller   : Yes...

Operator: ...That's...That's my address.

Caller   : Yes...

Operator: I'm – this – using 911 to play a joke –

Caller   : You can confirm my location. In fact, I'm sure you have by now.

報案室奇趣錄

接線員：這裏是 911 報案室，請問你的求助地址是？

來電者：我在牆壁裏。

接線員：先生，我要的是地址。

來電者：她不知道我在房子裏。

接線員：我需要知道你的具體情況。有人有危險嗎？

來電者：很快會有。

接線員：你可以告訴我發生甚麼事嗎？

來電者：我已經在這裏很久了，我一直在等，而我會繼續等下去。

接線員：先生，請你注意，打電話來 911 開玩笑是犯法行為。如果不是開玩笑，請你立即回答我。

來電者：不是玩笑，我躲了起來。

接線員：如果你不能提供你的位置，我會終止這通電話。

來電者：我在法爾茅斯山街 350 號。

接線員：⋯⋯先生？

來電者：是⋯⋯

接線員：⋯⋯那⋯⋯那是我的地址⋯⋯

來電者：是的⋯⋯

接線員：我⋯⋯這個⋯⋯打電話來 911 開玩笑⋯⋯

來電者：你可以確認我的位置，事實上，你現在也正在確認了吧。

Operator: Oh my God. (Inaudible)

Caller   : Yes.

Operator: Why are you doing this?

Caller   : When the wind is done blowing, never comes back.
            Destruction is its mausoleum.

Operator: That doesn't make any sense. Why are you in my
            house? Is something wrong there?

Caller   : Yes.

Operator: What's wrong?

Caller   : I am.

Operator: This – I don't understand.

Caller   : I watch you.

Operator: What?

Caller   : I live in your house and I watch you. I'm in the
            walls.

Operator: No.

Caller   : Yes.

Operator: (Inaudible)

Caller   : Speak up, Alice.

Operator: How do you know my name?

Caller   : I know more than you understand, Alice.

Operator: (Sobbing noise)

Caller   : Keep control, Alice.

Operator: Police are on their way.

Caller   : I know.

接線員：我的天啊⋯⋯（聲音不清）

來電者：是的。

接線員：你為甚麼要這樣做？

來電者：當猛風不再呼嘯，不再回歸，摧毀就是它的陵墓。

接線員：不可能的，你為甚麼會在我家？那裏有甚麼事嗎？

來電者：是的。

接線員：發生了甚麼事？

來電者：我。

接線員：這⋯⋯我搞不懂⋯⋯

來電者：我看守著你。

接線員：甚麼？

來電者：我住在你家裏，看守著你。我在牆壁裏。

接線員：不是的。

來電者：是的。

接線員：（聲音不清）

來電者：説大聲點，Alice。

接線員：你怎麼知道我的名字？

來電者：我比你想像中更加了解你啊，Alice。

接線員：（啜泣聲）

來電者：保持克制，Alice。

接線員：警方正趕到現場。

來電者：我知道。

Operator: You're committing a crime.

Caller : I know.

Operator: You'll be going to jail.

Caller : I doubt it.

Operator: Why?

Caller : You must realize, Alice, that I possess quite a bit of stealth. I'll be long gone by the time Unit 45 arrives from its location 1.2 miles away.

Operator: How…?

Caller : They'll see where I've been. They'll even figure out where I've been getting into and out of the walls.

Operator: Then stay away. Just stay away.

Caller : I will.

Operator: Good.

Caller : For a bit.

Operator: (Inaudible) Never. Never come back.

Caller : I'll return when you get complacent. You'll be alert, paranoid even, for some time – an emotional wreck who jumps at shadows. Justifiably so. Your family and friends will walk you through it. But slowly… you'll start to heal. Those aforementioned family and friends will support this healing. They'll encourage you to put this all behind, to move on. Once you've healed, after you've moved on, then I will return.

接線員：你這樣做等同犯罪。

來電者：我知道。

接線員：你要坐牢了。

來電者：可能不會喔。

接線員：為甚麼？

來電者：你發現了吧，Alice，我可以隱身，讓你不會發現到我。當四十五小隊在 1.2 英里的距離外來到你家時，我早已逃之夭夭。

接線員：你怎麼⋯⋯？

來電者：他們會發現我之前的藏身之處，甚至會查明我如何從牆壁裏進出。

接線員：那走吧，離開。

來電者：好的。

接線員：很好。

來電者：離開一點兒。

接線員：（聲音不清）以後，以後都不要再回來。

來電者：當你沾沾自喜的時候，我就會回來。你會有一陣子很警覺，甚至會疑神疑鬼，心情很差，卻欣然接受了陰影，這樣也很合理。你的家人和朋友會與你一起共渡難關。漸漸地，你會開始療傷，並且好起來，之前提及過的那些家人朋友會很支持你療傷，鼓勵你忘記過去，重新振作。當你療傷過後，振作過後，我就會回來。

Operator: (Inaudible)

Caller   : It's better this way. Healing will be your pain.

Operator: I'll move.

Caller   : I'll follow.

Operator: (Inaudible)

Caller   : Surely you must comprehend that if I know so much, nothing you do happens without my knowledge. You'll never be free. The wonderful thing is that even when I'm physically away, I'll always be on your mind. I'll never leave.

Operator: (Inaudible)

Caller   : Good night, Alice.

接線員：（聲音不清）

來電者：這樣對你比較好，療傷會令你更痛苦。

接線員：我會搬走。

來電者：我會跟隨。

接線員：（聲音不清）

來電者：你應該理解到我真的很了解你吧，你的一舉一動我
　　　　都瞭如指掌。你不可能自由了。這件事的美妙之處
　　　　在於，即使我肉體不在你身邊，我也一直都會在你
　　　　腦海裏，永遠不會離開。

接線員：（聲音不清）

來電者：晚安，Alice。

My Daughter is a Sensitive Child

She's such a socially awkward child, my daughter. And sensitive, too. I can never come right out and tell her to do or not to do something. It makes her too upset, as if I've scolded her.

I've recently tried to go the old-fashioned story telling route. Before bed every night, I tell her a story with a moral. Maybe it's a story about a lonely teddy bear who wouldn't share or a story about a pony who wouldn't speak up in class. This seems to be the gentlest way of getting the point across to her. Last night I made a mistake. All day long as I talked to her, I watched in growing frustration as her eyes darted around the room, looking everywhere but at me. That night I scooped her up in my arms and carried her to bed. I tucked her in tight and sat down next to her on the bed.

"Daddy, what's my story tonight?"
"Well, once upon a time there was a little girl."
"Like me?"
"Just like you. Now, this little girl was a very smart girl. But, she had a problem."
"What was it?"
"Well, I'll tell you. Whenever people spoke to this little girl, she wouldn't look at them. She'd look at the ceiling, or at the floor, or at a spot on the wall. One day, she was walking along in the woods when she came upon a witch. The witch said, oh

睡前故事

我女兒是個不太擅於交際的孩子，同時她也很敏感、很易受傷害。我不能直接跟她說她要做甚麼，或是不能做甚麼，否則她會覺得我是在罵她，她就會很難過。

我最近試著一個很老套的方法——說故事。每晚睡覺前，我都會跟她說一個有寓意的故事，例如一隻不願意分享的泰迪熊，或是一隻在課室說話很小聲的小馬等等。用這種方法教她，應該算是最溫和了吧。但是昨晚我搞砸了⋯⋯昨晚我跟她說話時，她總是四周張望，但就是不看著我，這使我很沮喪。於是我抱著她走進睡房，幫她蓋好被子，然後坐到她床邊開始說故事。

「爸爸，今晚說甚麼故事呢？」
「唔⋯⋯很久很久以前，有一個小女孩。」
「像我一樣的小女孩嗎？」
「是的，跟你一樣。那個小女孩很聰明，但是，她有個小毛病。」
「甚麼毛病？」
「就是呢，當別人跟她說話的時候，她都不會看著別人，她會看著天花板，看著地下，或是看著牆上的斑點。有一天，她在叢林著走著走著，碰到了一個女巫。女巫跟小女孩說：『噢！是個又乖又聰明的小女孩呢！』小女孩跟女巫道謝，但她說話時眼睛看著樹梢，沒有看著女巫，使女巫非常生

what a good and smart girl! The girl said thank you, but she was looking up at the tops of the trees. This made the witch very angry. She grabbed up the girl and sat her down in her hut. Why won't you look me in the eye, asked the witch? The girl said she didn't know. She was very scared. Finally, the witch got so angry that she went around the forest, scooping out the eyes of the woodland creatures. She made a crown of eyes and placed it on the girl's head, so that no matter where the witch stood, the girl could always be looking at her."

I looked down at my daughter, who was looking back at me, her eyes wide. I knew it then—I'd screwed up.

"But, of course, in real life, witches don't exist," I said, feeling ashamed of myself. She only nodded. I went to bed, fully expecting my daughter to come running into my room in the middle of the night, scared by nightmares that I'd fueled with my story. To my surprise, she didn't.

I saw why this morning when I woke up. There, on the kitchen table was a crown. The eyes were different colors and sizes, all woven together by a pink band of optic nerves. My daughter stood next to them, looking proud and fearful at the same time. She lifted her blood–stained hands toward me.

"I made it so that I can always look at you, Daddy."

氣。於是女巫把女孩抓了起來，把她帶回自己的小屋。『為甚麼你不望著我的眼睛？』女巫問道。快嚇壞的女孩回答說她不知道。女巫勃然大怒，跑到森林裏把動物的眼睛挖了出來，做了一個眼睛冠冕給小女孩，然後把它戴到小女孩的頭上。這樣無論女巫站在哪裏，小女孩都可以望到她了。」

我低頭望著女兒，她也瞪著眼睛回望著我。那時我知道自己搞砸了。

「但當然，在現實世界中，女巫是不存在的。」我羞愧地說。她只是點點頭，沒有說話。我也走回自己的房間睡覺了，滿心期待女兒會在半夜做惡夢，驚醒了跑過來找我，並撒嬌說故事太恐怖了。但出乎意料地，她沒有這樣做。

我今早醒來就知道了為甚麼，在廚房那邊，放著一個冠冕。那些眼睛全都是不同顏色和大小，粉紅色的視覺神經把它們編織在一起。我女兒站在旁邊，既驕傲卻又很膽怯的望著我，然後向我伸出她那血跡斑斑的雙手。

「爸爸，我弄了這個，這樣我就可以常常看著你了。」

The Recognition He Deserved

I suppose I should start by saying that, yes, I indeed murdered Ronald Randall. All those horrible things you saw on the news were done by my own hand. I will spare you the grislier details. No doubt you've probably heard about it from the media like everyone else.

People ask me why I killed Ronald, my best friend and most trusted companion. I'm afraid I must answer their question with a question: Before his death, had anyone ever heard of him? Or about his writings?

I'm not surprised if the answer was no. He was a great author, with inspiration that could only have come from the Muses themselves. His novels should have been recommended reading for any bibliophile.

But like many great men, his masterpieces were passed over for horrible writing and cheap titillation pushed out to the lowest common denominator of mankind.

I saw the crushing despair on his face as time and again his greatest works were ignored in favor of "bodice rippers" and "vampire paramours" and whatever literary trend the powers that be wanted to push out that month.

好朋友的承諾

我應該由這裏開始說起,是的,我確實是殺死了 Ronald Randall。你在新聞報導上看到的可怕事都是我親手幹的。我稍後會再詳述那些更恐怖的細節,不過你可能跟其他人一樣,早已從傳媒口中聽說過了。

他們問我 Ronald 既是我最好的朋友,也是我最信任的伙伴,那我為甚麼要殺掉他?恐怕我只好反問他們:「他在世的時候,你們聽過他的名字嗎?有讀過他的作品嗎?」

如果他們答我沒有,我也不會感到驚訝。Ronald 生前是個很出色的作家,他的腦袋簡直像是希臘神話中主司文學、藝術與科學的繆思女神們般,非常有智慧。每個藏書家都應該要閱讀,並且收藏他寫的小說。

但跟很多偉人一樣,大家都以為 Ronald 的作品是一些寫得很差、低俗又嘩眾取寵的爛作品,而忽略了那些作品其實是很出色的。

每當他的傑作不被重視時,他臉上都會掛著心碎絕望的表情。人們又再一次以為他寫的是情色作品,或是一些關於吸血鬼情人的故事,總之是那些權威學者不喜歡的文學潮流,因此沒有人留意到他的作品。

So when he confided in me that he was at his wit's end about it, I promised him I would do whatever it took to make his works known. We utilized all possible means of promoting his work, tried every method known to both of us. I even invested a significant amount of money into the ordeal. But no matter what we did, his works remained overlooked by all, Ronald's brilliance ignored for the same vapid and trite storytelling.

After seeing what the continuous soul–crushing rejections was doing to Ronald, I could bear it no further. I was willing to do anything to alleviate my best friend of his despair, no matter how dark and foul the deed would be.

So that night, I butchered him in his sleep. I did things to him that in any other light I would be horrified to even contemplate. But for Ronald, it was worth the dark stain on my soul.

The press did what I expected them to: They ate every bit of it up, and sensationalized the murder to the masses. And due to the all the infamy and scandal the crime attracted, people started to read his books for themselves. And just like when I had read them, they recognized the absolute genius that had gone unnoticed before.

所以當他向我訴苦，說他已經無計可施的時候，我向他保證我一定會竭盡所能，讓世人認識他的作品。我們施展渾身解數，用盡我們能想到的一切辦法來推廣他的作品，我甚至為這場苦戰投資了一大筆錢。但無論我們如何努力，還是沒有人注意到他的作品，大家的目光都只落在那些陳腔濫調的平庸故事。

望著 Ronald 不斷被拒絕，受盡折磨的他，靈魂似是逐漸被撕裂般，我再看不過眼了。無論那件事有多黑暗、有多污穢也好，只要可以讓我最好的朋友從絕望中解脫，我願意為他做任何事！

於是那晚我趁他睡著了，就狠狠地殺了他。我對他做的事實在是太可怕了，換著是其他情況，我根本連想也不敢想。縱使我的靈魂會因此印上不能磨滅的污點，但是為了Ronald，一切也是值得的。

那些新聞輿論的反應完全是正中下懷，他們很沉迷於我殺了Ronald 的事，更大肆渲染是次謀殺。這宗案件引起了不少罪惡和醜聞，反而吸引了人們去看他的書。人們翻閱他的作品時，反應跟我一樣，才發現自己原來一直以來都忽視了這顆聰明絕頂的滄海遺珠，紛紛驚訝不已。

It wasn't long before his past works became best–sellers. The cultural elite sing his praises from their ivory towers. The critics pour over his works, wondering how they hadn't noticed such beautiful storytelling before he had died. Publishers were fighting each other to gain the right to publish his last tale, finished only two days before his demise.

In death, Ronald Randall was finally getting the recognition and praise he truly deserved.

I had fulfilled the promise I had made to him.

And all it had cost was his life and my soul.

不久後，他的作品都成了暢銷書，連平時不吃人間煙火的文化精英都在歌頌他，那些評論家更爭相翻閱他的作品，驚嘆他們為甚麼在 Ronald 還在生的時候，沒有注意到他優雅的寫作手法。出版商也為他最後那本故事書的版權鬥得焦頭爛額，那是他離世前兩天剛剛完成的作品。

在九泉之下，Ronald Randall 終於得到他應有的認同和讚揚。

我已經履行了對他許下的承諾。

只不過代價是他的性命和我的靈魂而已。

He is Coming Again

Must be around five now. I'm not sure, wish there was a clock in my room. A noise outside. Mommy's car driving away. A shiver runs down my spine. This is it. Mom is gone again, which means I'm alone with... him. He'll come. Any moment now. Bastard, I won't let him. I won't put up with it anymore.

He's gonna hurt you. Shut your pie hole. If he hurts me again, I'm going to tell.

No you won't, you never did. I will too, shut up.

I can hear steps now, right outside the room. Instinctively, I pull the blanket closer to my body. It's getting hard to breath. Light's coming from beneath the door and I can see a pair of feet. Then, he knocked.

"Go away! You're not gonna do anything to me ever again, I hate you, I hate you! Go away!"

He tried to get in but I had blocked the door with a chair.

"Go away! I hate you Joshua, I hate you!"

But the chair wouldn't hold for long. He kicked the door, it slammed open.

他又來了

我猜，現在已經五點了，因為我房間沒有時鐘。外面有些聲音，那是媽媽駕車外出的聲音。突然，一股寒意顫慄全身。又是這樣了，媽媽又離開了，那就代表又只剩我跟他了……他又會隨時過來，防不勝防。混蛋，我不會讓他得逞的，我不會再忍受這樣的事了！

*他會傷害你的。*閉上你的臭嘴吧，如果他真的再傷害我的話，我會揭發他的。

*你不會的，你從來也沒有揭發過他。*我會的，你給我閉嘴。

我聽見房門外傳來了腳步聲。我本能地用被子蓋著自己，使我開始有點呼吸困難。燈光從門縫下透出來，我看見了一雙腳，然後他敲了敲門。

「走開！你不要再對我做任何事，我討厭你，很討厭你！走開啊！」

他想走進來，但我用椅子擋住了門，不讓他進來。

「走開！我討厭你，Joshua！我討厭你！」

但擋在門口的椅子熬不了多久，他一腳便踢開了房門。

"No!" I wrap myself in blankets. "If you hurt me I'm gonna tell!"

No you won't.

"Ms. Stevens, nobody is going to hurt you." Arms around me. I shake and fight as much as I can.

"Get out! Get out Joshua! I hate you!"
He doesn't like it when you call him that.

"Ms. Stevens, please!"
"No! You won't hurt me again! Leave me alone!"

A needle against my neck. My whole body goes numb. He grabs me, the blanket slips to the floor. He is carrying me away when I notice a window. Strange, it wasn't there before. Outside the window, a man carries an old lady as if she was a rag doll or something. Poor old lady.

That's not a window. Shut up. It is too.

「不要!」我躲進被窩裏,「如果你傷害我的話,我會揭發你的!」

你不會的。

「Stevens 女士,沒有人會傷害你。」有人環抱著我,我邊發抖邊盡力掙脫著。

「出去!Joshua,出去!我討厭你!」

他不喜歡你這樣說他的。

「Stevens 女士,冷靜一點!」
「不要!你不要再傷害我!別煩我!」

有根針刺進了我的脖子,使我四肢乏力。他把我抓了起來,被子掉在地上。他帶走我的同時,我看見了一個窗戶。真奇怪,之前明明沒有這個窗戶的。窗外那個男人拖著個老太太,好像拖著個洋娃娃般。真是個可憐的老太太。

*那不是窗戶。*閉嘴,那肯定是窗戶。

"Mr. Stevens, I'm afraid your mom's condition is deteriorating."

The doctor looks at me with a mix of sorrow and professionalism. I shake my head in silence, not knowing what to answer. He goes on.

"Her... episodes are getting more violent. She seems to be reviving a traumatic experience on a daily basis, be it real or made up."
"Isn't there anything you can do to make her better?"
"I assure you, we are trying. But this is the thing with Alzheimer's, eventually there's nothing that can be done anymore. There is one thing, though. Do you know anyone by the name 'Joshua'?"

That was a strange question.

"Sure, it's my grandfather's name. Her dad. Well, stepdad actually. Why?"
"Were there ever traumatic events in your mother's life, involving this man?"
"No, of course not. I mean, if there were, she never told anyone."
"I see. We'll keep you informed, Mr. Stevens. Thank you for your time."

「Stevens 先生，恐怕你母親的病情每況愈下了。」

醫生望著我的眼神帶點哀傷，卻又不失專業。我無語地搖著頭，不知該怎麼回答。他繼續說下去。

「她的片段……愈來愈激烈了，那些創傷似乎每天也在重複上演著。不論那些畫面是事實還是虛構，似乎對她造成了很大傷害。」
「你能做點甚麼讓她好過一點嗎？」
「我向你保證我們正盡力協助她。但這樣的事在老人痴呆症患者身上很常見，最後可能做甚麼也是徒然。不過有一件事想問你，你有認識的人叫 Joshua 嗎？」

這問題真奇怪。

「有啊，我爺爺就是叫 Joshua，也就是她爸爸。呃，正確來說是繼父。怎麼了嗎？」
「你母親受到精神創傷的經歷會否跟這位先生有關？」
「不會，當然不會。我是說，就算真的有關的話，她也沒有跟任何人提起過。」
「明白。Stevens 先生，有消息的話我們會再通知你。感謝你寶貴的時間。」

Vicious Revenge
辣 手 報 復

Natural Born Killer

Billy had always been a pain in my ass. He whined non stop and did nothing but leech off me and my boyfriend. That's why I killed him. It was easier than I thought it would be. I just walked up and split his head open with a baseball bat. After that, it was simple matter of taking a bunch of things to make it look like a robbery.

You mustn't think poorly of me; I would never deliberately harm another human being. Billy and his kind were parasites though, never contributing, never helping, just lazing about taking up resources that could be used for real people.

I know my boyfriend wouldn't understand though, he was clearly fond of Billy. To divert any suspicions I went to Billy's funeral with him. It was going fine until they brought in the coffin. At the sight of it, my boyfriend and I both hid our faces in our hands. Him to hide his tears and me to hide my shock.

I didn't think they would bury Billy in a full sized coffin, after all, I had just given birth to him two months ago.

天生殺人狂

Billy 一直以來也是我的眼中釘，他一天到晚也在哭鬧，不幹實事，只懂依賴我和我男朋友。於是我殺了他，這回事比我想像中輕鬆得多。我只是走過去，用棒球棍把他的頭一分為二而已。在那之後，我只需要把東西翻亂，營造被盜竊的感覺就行了，非常簡單。

你先不要把我想得那麼壞，我是絕對不會蓄意傷害其他人的。但 Billy 和他的同類簡直像寄生蟲般，毫無貢獻、遊手好閒，只顧懶洋洋地浪費著地球資源。

我知道我男朋友是不會明白的，因為他顯然是很喜歡 Billy。為了不想引起嫌疑，我跟男朋友一起出席了 Billy 的喪禮。喪禮一切進行得很順利，直至工作人員把棺材拿出來……一看到這個畫面，我和男朋友都用雙手掩著臉。他掩飾著自己流淚，我則掩飾著自己的震驚。

我沒想過他們會用成人大小的棺材來埋葬 Billy，因為我兩個月前才把他生下來啊。

Mandatory Euthanasia

"With the passing of the newest ordinance, all citizens deemed to be not of permissive mental or physical ability will hereby be subjected to immediate and mandatory euthanasia."

The first wave of killings went mostly unnoticed. At first, the government came only for those with severe mental impairments, the ones who were already hidden away in sanatoriums and forgotten. Naively, we thought that the executions would end there.

We were wrong. The prime minister's vision of a perfect world had evolved. Now included in his criteria for euthanasia were **any individual possessing a physical handicap that inhibited their ability to contribute to the workforce.** The blind, the deaf, the paralysed– an entire swath of the population were now scheduled for death.

Being a highly respected figure in my field of work, I had hoped against hope that we could somehow bribe our way out of this. Unfortunately, any delusion that social standing would be enough to protect my family was shattered when they showed up at our doorstep. **No exemptions from mandatory euthanasia would be made based on communal status.**

Jenny showed nothing but grace in our final moments

強制性安樂死

「隨著最新條例通過，所有精神或身體功能有障礙的公民將要接受即時及強制性的安樂死。」

第一波的屠殺幾乎無聲無息的結束了。最初政府只是除去那些患有嚴重的精神障礙的人，他們大多都在療養院過著隱蔽的生活，已經沒有人記得他們了。我們天真地以為被屠殺的「人選」只僅於此。但我們錯了。

首相時常憧憬著一個完美的世界，於是他現在又制定了一個新規則：**「任何人士因身體殘障導致工作能力減退或無法工作，將要接受安樂死。」**那些視障、聽障，以及癱瘓的人士，這個人數眾多的群體現在正排期準備被處決。

我在業界是位德高望重的前輩，對於政府這樣的安排，我仍然相信有一線生機。我本以為我的社會地位足以保障家人的安危，但不幸地，當他們在我家門口出現時，我才發現我甚麼也保不住了。**在強制性安樂死這個公共的社會規範下，沒有人可以成為例外。**

Jenny 帶著感恩的心和我們一起度過最後時刻。坐在輪椅上的她把自己推到門前，冷靜而又衷心的向家人道別。自從我的寶貝女兒發生意外之後，我看著她成長了很多，即使四肢癱瘓了也努力生存，把難題一一擊破。但這一切即將結束。

together. She wheeled herself to the door and bid a heartfelt but steady goodbye to her family members. I had watched my beautiful daughter accomplish so much since her accident, pull herself up from the struggles of quadriplegia and fight to exist. All for it to end here.

"No one among us is invincible" she would tell schoolchildren while campaigning for road safety. *"Accidents happen all the time."* My Jenny inspired me, inspired all of us, so greatly.

As fate would have it, events soon brought the prime minister into my life. A simple, routine operation was all he needed. For this, the prime minister wanted the best neurosurgeon in the nation. It made sense. Operations around the spinal cord are very dangerous, with so many potential risks and complications.

While I prepped for surgery, I began to wonder if perhaps there was value in the government's plan to purge the nation of the disabled. As cruel as it seems, I could now see how killing those who weigh society down may indeed be what society needs to move forward. Maybe mandatory euthanasia really was the way. Behind my surgical mask, I smiled for the first time in months.

No one among us is invincible. Accidents happen all the time.

「*我們不是無敵的，*」她在教導那些學童道路安全時會這樣說：「*而意外總是難免的。*」我親愛的 Jenny 啟發了我很多，也大大啟發了我們所有人。

似是命中注定般，首相先生在我的生命裏出現了。雖然以他的病情來說，他只需要一個簡單的常規手術，但首相先生要求全國最頂尖的神經外科醫生來替他施手術。他這樣想也不無道理的，因為在脊椎附近進行手術的確非常危險，而且隱藏著很多潛在風險，也有機會引起併發症。

當我在準備手術的事宜時，我在想，政府把那些殘障的人們殺掉來淨化國家，實行這樣的計劃會不會其實是值得的呢？雖然這樣似乎很殘忍，但我現在覺得，把那些在社會上舉足輕重的權貴殺掉，好像才是讓社會進步的好方法。強制性安樂死可能真的有效。戴著外科用口罩的我，展露著多個月以來的第一個笑容。

我們不是無敵的，而意外總是難免的嘛。

A Good Wife

Elnora Carroll shivered and turned out the light by the bed. It always seemed cold in the house these days, even with the woodstove roaring and all her quilts piled on the bed. Ever since Jack had died in that terrible way last month, she could never get warm.

It had been an accident, though. She just hadn't heard him call after he fell. And the poor man froze to death right out in his own yard....

"It could've happened to anyone." she thought sleepily. *"I just didn't hear him."*

"I was a good wife to him for years. I'd never...." but the thought trailed off into an uneasy sleep.

The scratching was what woke her, a couple hours later. Scratching at the front door...

"Wha—?" she sat bolt upright.

Scratch—scraaaaaaatch—It was unearthly and insistent, and sent an icy chill through her.

"Raccoon? Or possum?" she thought, and tried to huddle back under the covers.

賢妻

Elnora Carroll 發著抖，關掉了床頭燈。在這段日子裏，無論壁爐的火燒得多旺，蓋上了多少張被子也好，房子還是很冷。自從上個月 Jack 離世之後，她就再沒有溫暖過。

他死得很慘，但那只是個意外，他跌倒之後，她沒有聽見他求救，結果那個可憐的男人就在自己的院子裏活活凍死。

「*這些事誰也有可能遇到吧⋯⋯*」她睡眼惺忪地想著：「*我只是沒有聽見他求救而已⋯⋯*」

「*跟他結婚了這麼多年，我一直都是個賢內助，我從來也沒有⋯⋯*」她懷著忐忑不安的心情，想著想著就睡著了。

幾個小時之後，一些抓門聲把她吵醒了。那些抓門聲是從前門傳來的⋯⋯

「甚麼⋯⋯？」她嚇得坐直了身子。

*嘰吱──嘰嘰嘰吱──*持續不斷的抓門聲，聽起來很怪異，嚇得她毛骨悚然。

「*是浣熊？還是負鼠？*」她邊想，邊縮回被子裏面。

Scraaaaatch again, this time outside her window. Elnora shook under the covers, terrified.

"I was a good wife; he wouldn't haunt me", she thought frantically, trying to push the idea out of her mind.

The scratching, dragging sounds were inside the house now, slowly approaching the bedroom....

"Jack, you go away! I was a good wife! I never heard you call for help! Go away!" she cried, desperately afraid....

But in the door he came, anyway, her dead husband, ashy blue and frozen, dragging himself along the floor towards her...

Asking in his dead cold voice, as he grabbed at her throat, "If you didn't hear me call, then how do you know I ever called?"

嘰嘰嘰吱——又來了，這次是從窗戶那邊傳來。Elnora 在被窩裏發抖，怕得要命。

「*我是個賢妻，他不會這樣騷擾我的。*」這個想法卻在腦海中縈繞不斷，幾乎迫瘋了她。

那些抓刮聲、拖曳聲現在移到房子裏面了，而且慢慢地靠近 Elnora 的睡房……

「Jack，你走開吧！我是個賢妻！我真的沒有聽見你在求救！走開！」她絕望地哭喊著。

但睡房門還是打開了，她已故的丈夫走了進來，呈灰藍色、凍僵的他緩慢而吃力的爬向她……

他掐著她的脖子，冷冷地問道：「你說沒有聽見我求救對吧？那你怎麼會知道我曾經求救過？」

It's a Small Town

They woke me up, the god damn bastards. First good night of sleep I have in years and they woke me up. I knew they'd come, but this soon? Risked a peek through the window. The street down there was trashed from the previous night. Candy packages everywhere, toilet paper rolls, pieces of candy. God dammit those kids.

It's a small town, y'know. Very small. The kind of town where you'll get angry looks from overprotective parents if you refuse to take part in this pathetic little ritual of theirs. The kind of town where they'll question whether you're good enough to be a teacher if you won't participate in this senseless tradition of feeding sugar to their greasy infants once a year.

The thought of it makes me want to puke. "Trick or treat", yeah right. "Extortion" is what they call it in courts.

I've refused to take part on that nonsense. Look at them. Grown men and women, some still wearing last night's costumes. I bet they get off on leaving the house like that. Todd Jacobs is dressed like a vampire, wow, really creative Todd. Hannah Mitchells is some colorful–haired character from some stupid superhero movie. She was crying now and the mascara rolled down her face. Heh, funny.

小鎮大事

那些該死的混蛋吵醒了我。這是我多年以來終於可以安睡的一晚，他們竟然吵醒了我！我知道他們會來的，但也太早了吧？我冒險地向窗外瞥了一眼，整條街都佈滿了人們昨晚留下的垃圾，到處也是糖果包裝紙、廁紙筒，還有一顆顆散落地上的糖果。那些天殺的臭小子。

這只是個小鎮，很小的鎮。在這樣的鎮子裏，如果你不參與這個可悲小習俗的話，那些過度保護孩子的家長便會向你目露兇光；在這樣的鎮子裏，如果你不參與這每年一度的白痴傳統，不肯餵糖給那些滿身脂肪的孩童的話，他們就會懷疑你能否勝任老師一職。

這樣的想法簡直讓我想吐。「不給糖就搗蛋」，對吧，也就是在法庭上所指的「敲詐勒索罪」。

我不肯參與這個荒謬的活動。你看看他們，大家都是成年人了，有些還穿著昨晚的戲服，我肯定他們出門時就已經穿成這個模樣了。Todd Jacobs 穿了吸血鬼裝，嗚哇，非常創新呢，Todd！Hannah Mitchells 則扮演超級英雄電影裏的蠢蛋角色，把頭髮弄得五顏六色的。現在還哭得睫毛膏都化掉了，變成兩道黑線掛在她臉上。嘻嘻，真有趣！

Someone spotted me watching through the window and threw a rock at it. The glass shattered. They were screaming their lungs off. This was serious, oh boy, I hate this town so much. They punched the door, more of them arriving at each second. Twenty of 'em, no, thirty... was that the sheriff?

The door would give in any time now. All because I didn't wanna take part on their precious tradition, all because they couldn't accept that someone was different. I ran to the basement just as the door fell. That mob of senseless monsters got in. I opened the fridge and picked up the beaker glass. It looked like water with a tiny bit of smoke floating around in it. I could feel my shirt moving as my heart pounded beneath it.

Yes, I've refused to take part. Refused to even open the door to those spiteful children.

I refused... last year. And they made me pay for it. This time, though, I had learned my lesson. I did it, I took part, but still here they were.

Angry, mad, crying.

They stormed the basement just as I emptied the beaker. My whole body trembled and I was suddenly shaking on the floor.

有人發現了我在窗邊窺看，丟了塊石頭過來，玻璃立即碎滿一地。他們聲嘶力竭地尖叫著。這很嚴重喔！哎呀，我真的很討厭這個鎮子。他們捶打著我的門，走過來的人每秒也在增加。二十幾個，不，三十……那是警長嗎？

那道門隨時捱不住了。只是因為我不想參與他們那珍而重之的傳統而已；只是因為他們接受不了有人跟他們不一樣而已。門倒下的瞬間，我跑進了地下室，而那些像洪水猛獸的鄰居們就闖進了我的房子。我打開冰箱，拿了個燒杯出來，那些液體看起來像微微冒煙的水。我心跳快得彷彿使我的襯衫也跟著動起來了。

是的，我不肯參與，甚至那些惡毒的孩子過來敲門，我也不肯開門。

我不願意參與，但那是上年的事，他們要我付出代價。不過今次我學乖了，我參與了！但他們還是闖進來了。

每個人都怒不可遏、暴跳如雷、淚流滿面。

他們猛攻進地下室之際，燒杯剛好空了。我全身發抖，下一秒就倒在地上抽搐著。其實不應該一次服下這麼多的，應該只服很少的劑量。這樣的話，藥力大約在六小時後才會生

You're not supposed to take so much at once. You gotta take a very small dose. This way, it will take about six hours before acting. But when it acts, it's a matter of seconds.

Small doses.

Just like the ones I slipped inside the candies.

效。但一旦生效，則只消幾秒時間。

低劑量。

就像我混進糖果裏的那般。

They Called Me Elephant Man

For as long as I can remember, my head has been this way.

When I was a child, my parents took me from specialist to specialist in search of a cure. All we knew for certain was that my head had swollen to the point where I more resembled a bobblehead than a human. Word quickly spread throughout the medical community. The consensus was that I had Neurofibromatosis Type 1– making me a modern–day Elephant Man. Only one person, a faith healer, seemed to think any different. Upon seeing me, she immediately dismissed NF1 as the cause of my deformity.

"You, my child, are no 'Elephant Man'" the healer said, amused. "One day you will understand why. One day you will understand your true nature."

Despite my mystery ailment, I never let my appearance hold me back. I was a naturally social child and, thankfully, the kids in my community were understanding enough to look past my condition. As I grew up, I continued to meet open–minded people who embraced me for who I was inside. It gave me hope that one day I could teach the world the value in looking different. Shortly after graduation, I finally fulfilled my dream. Before I knew it, I was one town over, on the stage of my first–ever motivational speaking gig. I had spoken publicly about my condition before, in front of classmates

我不是象人

自有記憶以來，我的頭一直都是這個模樣。

小時候，爸媽為了治好我，帶我看過很多個不同的專家。但我們只知道我的頭腫了起來，腫到一個地步，使我看起來像個搖頭娃娃，而不像個人類。我的個案很快傳遍了醫學界。他們一致認為我患有神經纖維瘤一型，使我成了現代的象人。卻有一個人不認同那些專家的說法，她是個信仰治療師，她接見我後，就馬上否定了我畸形的頭部是因為患上纖維瘤所致。

「孩子，你不是象人。」治療師愉快的說著：「終有一天你會知道這句話的意思，終有一天你會知道你的本性。」

儘管患上了怪病，但我從來不會因為自己的外表而拖自己後腿。我是個有正常社交的孩子，而且社區內的孩子都很善解人意，不介意我的病情，讓我很感恩。到我漸漸長大，我遇到的所有人思想都很開放，他們會因為我的內在而欣然接受我。這些經歷使我充滿信心，希望將來有一天，可以以一個「外表與眾不同」的身份，跟世人分享我的價值觀。畢業後不久，我終於實現了夢想！當時我身處鄰鎮，我才獲悉有人邀請我上台，做我人生中第一個勵志演講。雖然我之前有跟同學分享過，也有在訪問中公開談及過我的病情，但這次的

and interviewers. But this crowd was different.

Throughout my speech, they jeered, sniggered and pointed. Every attempt to engage them was met with cruel retorts. The final blow came in the form of a rotting melon against the side of my skull. Delighted, the crowd erupted with laughter. I had never felt humiliation like this before. It dawned on me that this entire event had been a joke, a cheap way to get a freak onstage to deride. I couldn't fathom that people like this still existed, that nothing in the past century had changed.

As my hysteria began to grow, so too did my head. I could feel the undulating folds and flaps of my face drawing outwards, doubling and then tripling in size. The audience cowered before my massive head, which now towered over a pit of waiting flesh. Seconds before my jaw unhinged, it finally occurred to me what the faith healer had meant.

I am, indeed, no Elephant Man.

Elephants are herbivores.

觀眾不一樣。

在我演說期間，他們嘲弄、竊笑著我，又對我指手劃腳。我很努力嘗試令觀眾們投入一點，但每每只有殘忍的拒絕。他們甚至丟了一個腐爛的蜜瓜過來，打中我的頭。他們即時被逗樂了，全部人都哈哈大笑了起來。我從來沒有這樣被人羞辱過。我頓悟原來整個活動只是場鬧劇，他們只是隨便找個怪胎上台來當笑柄。原來現在還有這樣的人，簡直難以置信！原來即使時代進步了，他們也沒有進步過。

隨著我的怒氣飆升，我的頭也愈長愈大。我感覺到臉上那些像波浪般的皺摺向外伸展著，體積更以倍數增長著。我的頭長得像個高塔般，使台下的觀眾都蜷縮在我巨型的頭之下。甫在我張開嘴巴之前數秒，我才明白信仰治療師那句話的玄機。

的確，我不是象人。

大象是草食性動物。

You Never Call, You Never Write...

David unfolded the letter gingerly, trying not to touch it any more than he had to. God, why couldn't she just leave him alone? But no....

My Dear Son,
How are you? I never see you anymore. Are you getting my letters? I never hear from you, and nobody tells me anything here....

Blah, blah, blah. Fucking old bat. Why couldn't she just die already?

I'm hungry a lot here. I don't think they bring meals as often as they should, but you know how forgetful I am...maybe I just eat and then forget I ate.

Forgetful? Fucking senile, more like it. But then, she'd been a terrible mother when he was young – with her string of ever–changing boyfriends, going out drinking and God knew what else, leaving David locked in the house....

And there had *never* been enough to eat–bags of chips, maybe, or a fucking Happy Meal, when she remembered in her alcohol–addled brain that she had a child to feed. But now she was the one locked up, having to wait for someone who may or may not remember to bring her a meal, or clean up after her. Too senile to realize she was in her own

音訊全無

David 小心翼翼地打開信件，根本不想多碰它一下。天啊，難道她就不能放過他嗎？但是……

親愛的兒子，
你好嗎？已經很久沒有見過你了。你有收到我的信嗎？已經很久沒有聽見你的消息了，這裏也沒有人跟我說話……

諸如此類的廢話。他媽的老而不，她不能快點去死嗎？

我在這邊快要餓壞了。我覺得他們好像愈來愈少送餐過來，但你知道我有多健忘吧……可能我已經吃過東西了，但過了一會兒又會忘記自己原來已經吃飽了。

健忘？哼，老糊塗才對吧。以前在 David 還年輕的時候，她都不曾是個稱職的母親，她的事跡多不勝數，例如換男朋友如換衣服、出去喝酒（天曉得她還做了甚麼糟糕事）、把 David 鎖在家中……

而且家中食物永遠都不夠，有時候被酒浸壞了腦袋的她，突然想起自己原來有個小孩要餵養，才可能會買幾包薯片，或是買一個他媽的開心樂園餐回來給 David 吃。但現在被鎖在家的人是她，等待著有人記起，或者記不起要送餐給她，等待著有人會替她收拾乾淨。甚至糊塗得意識不到她正身處自

bedroom, instead of the senior home.

Too senile to realize she was being slowly starved to death....

David refolded the letter and stuffed it back into its envelope, re-sealing it carefully. He took out a pen, and wrote "**ADDRESSEE UNKNOWN–RETURN TO SENDER**" on it, and shoved it back under his mother's locked bedroom door.

己的睡房，而不是老人院。

糊塗得意識不到自己將會慢慢餓死……

David 重新摺好信件，放回原本的信封，謹慎地把封口重新封好。他拿起筆，寫上「**查無此人，退回寄件者**」，然後把信塞到他母親那鎖著的睡房門下。

Not Like Other Girls

Josh swept Laura's coat off of her shoulders and hung it in the closet. "Here we are." Smiling at her with affection, he inquired, "Wine?"

She nodded. He paused, holding her gently. "You know, you're not like other girls, Laura." There was a tender kiss on her forehead, and he left.

Laura watched him go. Over the last five months, she'd come to believe that he genuinely adored her, which made her happy. His adoration was all she wanted.

The sound of clanging metal erupted from the kitchen, followed by a cheerful "Whoops!" from Josh. Laura chuckled as she went into the den and made herself comfortable on the couch.

While she waited, she heard a tinkling noise coming from the closet. She looked towards the kitchen, assuming Josh would come in any second. He didn't. The tinkling persisted.

Laura scanned the room, and hesitantly approached the closet door. The knob was old and required a good strong twist, but she was able to get it open.

不像其他女生

Josh 替 Laura 脫掉外套，掛到衣櫃裏。「終於來到這裏了，」他情深款款地微笑問道：「喝酒嗎？」

她點點頭。他止住了動作，溫柔地抱著她說：「Laura，你知道嗎？你不像其他女生啊。」他輕吻了她額頭一下，才轉身離開。

Laura 看著他離去，回想著這五個月以來，她一直都希望可以得到他衷心的愛慕，現在願望成真了，她很高興，她渴望的正是他的愛慕。

廚房傳來了金屬碰撞的叮叮噹噹聲，接著是 Josh 樂呵呵的叫道：「哎呀！」Laura 笑了笑，然後走到了活動室，舒適地躺在沙發上。

Laura 等待的期間，她聽見衣櫃裏傳來了「哐啷」一聲。她向前望望廚房，猜想 Josh 應該很快過來了吧。但他還未過來，而那些哐啷聲仍然響個不停。

Laura 環顧整個房間後，戰戰兢兢地走近衣櫃門。雖然衣櫃的門把很老舊，要花很大的氣力才能扭開，Laura 還是成功把衣櫃打開了。

She was greeted by an unexpectedly musty smell…and an unmistakable breeze, wafting towards her from behind the coats and knick–knacks in the closet. Curious and surprised, she pushed the coats to the side and gaped when a set of stairs was revealed.

The tinkling continued, louder now.

Laura looked behind her cautiously. Once she'd verified Josh was still in the kitchen, she noticed a light switch on the wall. She flicked it on and descended the stairs.

The tinkling grew louder yet.

Laura stared in horror.

Chained to the wall were four women. Dried blood was caked around their wrists and ankles. Three were unconscious (she hoped) and hung limply. One was awake, but barely. She weakly moved her arms, causing the tinkling.

Before she could move, there was a voice in her ear.

"See, Laura, I told you you're not like other girls," Josh said. "None of the others were as dumb—"

撲面而來的竟是一股發霉味，而且她肯定有陣微風從衣櫃裏的外套和小擺設後面吹出來。Laura 既好奇又驚訝，於是把那些外套撥到一邊，一道樓梯頓時出現在眼前，嚇呆了她。

哐啷聲沒有停止，現在甚至更大聲了。

Laura 謹慎地望向自己後方，確認了 Josh 還在廚房，回頭之際就看到了牆上有個燈掣。她把燈開了，然後走下樓梯。

哐啷聲愈來愈大聲。

映入眼簾的景象使 Laura 驚恐不已……

四個女人被人用鐵鏈鎖在牆上，她們的手腕和腳踝滿是乾掉的血痕。其中三個女人昏迷了（她希望是），癱軟地懸吊在半空。還有一個是清醒的，但也很勉強，她虛弱地擺動著手臂，原來那些哐啷聲就是她弄的。

她還未動身，就有一把聲音傳入她的耳朵。

「看吧，Laura，我就說你不像其他女生吧，」Josh 說：「她們都不像你那麼笨……」

His words were cut off by an elbow to the face. He staggered back to the stairs, just in time for Laura to land a blow to his skull with a fireplace poker.

Laura stood over the prone figure, a look of disgust on her face. Five months of pretending to care about this fuckface, five months of concealing her true motives, just to get access to this room.

She went to the conscious woman, opened the manacles. Held her when she fell to her knees, emaciated and weak.

"It's okay now, sis," Laura said softly. "I'm here."

Laura 用手肘狠狠擊向 Josh 的臉，打斷了他的話。他搖搖晃晃地退到樓梯口，就在此時，Laura 用壁爐火鉗猛轟在他的腦袋上。

Laura 站在那趴著的軀體旁邊，回想起五個月以來一直在裝很關心這個混蛋，使她一臉厭惡。這五個月以來，她一直在掩飾自己真正的動機——來到他的房間。

她走向那個清醒的女人，並解開她的手銬。Laura 上前抱著那個又瘦又弱的女人，免得她跪倒在地上。

「妹妹，現在沒事了，」Laura 溫柔地說：「姊姊在這裏。」

A Mother's Love

"Mother, you can't keep doing this!"

I've lost track of how many times I've told her. By phone. By e—mail. In person. I keep telling her I'm not that shy, quiet child that gets picked on by everyone. I'm a grown man now, complete with a job and college degree! I can fight my own battles.

"She hurt you, child. They all did." Mother replies, handing me a piece of pie and humming along to the song on the radio. Apple pie, my favorite. "What kind of mother would I be if I didn't do something?"

I know mother still sees me as her sweet, innocent child, running to her when the bullies mess with me. She's never stopped me from doing whatever I wanted, but I know if she had her way, I'd be forever nearby. When she went too far and we lost my older brother, it just made her cling harder onto me – make sure that nothing ever hurt me. I know she was afraid of what might happen if she wasn't there to protect me.

"I know. I know." I say, taking the pie. She's not wrong. It hurt when I caught my girlfriend and my best friend…in my own bed, no less! Apparently, all my so—called "friends" knew about it and didn't tell me. If it wasn't for mother being there,

母親的愛

「媽媽，你不可以再這樣了！」

我已經數不清跟她說過多少遍，在電話裏說過、電郵裏說過，也面對面親口說過。我不斷告訴她，我不是她想的那個害羞、安靜、會被大家欺負的孩子。我已經長大成人了，而且有大學學位和工作，有能力自己解決困難了！

「乖孩子，她傷害了你啊，他們全部都傷害過你。」媽媽回答道。她把一塊餡餅遞給我，嘴巴哼唱著收音機播的歌。唔，是我最愛的蘋果餡餅！「如果我甚麼都不做，我還稱得上是個好媽媽嗎？」

我知道媽媽仍然把我當成一個可愛天真的小孩，她認為如果有人欺負我，我還是會跑到她身邊求助。她從來不會阻止我去做想做的事，但我知道如果她固執己見的話，我還是會永遠待在她身邊。她做得太過火了，令我失去了哥哥，從此她對我更加呵護備至，確保不會有任何事物傷害到我。我知道她是在擔心，要是沒有她保護我的話，我可能會有甚麼危險。

「是的，是的。」我邊吃著餡餅邊說。她沒有錯，那時候我真的很心痛。我撞破了女朋友和我最好的朋友……還要在我的床上！很明顯我那些所謂的「朋友」都是知情者，但他們

I'm not sure what I would have done. It probably wouldn't have been pretty, though.

"I just don't want you to get in trouble, mother. What if someone finds out?" I ask, grabbing a fork. "I'm just afraid if they ever catch you..."

Mother smiles in amusement. "You know I've always been careful. They didn't catch me back when Rodney broke your glasses. Or when that little strumpet stood you up at the Christmas dance. Or when Chad..."

"...taped me to the goalposts." I smiled as I remember what mother did after that. Not even the hometown football quarterback stood a chance against my mother when she put her mind to it. And where the heck did she find eels in Iowa?

"And if they didn't catch me then, they won't catch me now. Those fancy police computers have nothing on good ol' fashioned American know–how."

I suppose I should be more grateful. What other mother would do what mine does for me?

Mother turns down the radio and I hear it, coming faintly up from the floorboards; screams. My ex–girlfriend's scream.

全都沒有告訴我。如果不是因為媽媽也在現場，我不知道自己會做出甚麼事來，雖然應該是甚麼都不會做。

「我不想媽媽你惹到甚麼麻煩而已，如果被人發現了怎麼辦？」我拿著叉子問道：「我擔心他們會注意到⋯⋯」

媽媽微笑著跟我說：「你知道我一向非常謹慎吧，Rodney弄壞你的眼鏡時沒人發現；又或是那個小婊子在聖誕舞會放你鴿子時也沒有人發現；或者當 Chad⋯⋯」

「⋯⋯用膠帶把我綁在龍門柱上也沒有人發現。」我回想起媽媽當時為我做了些甚麼，不禁微笑了起來。當我媽媽立定決心的時候，就連那個四分衛也敵不過她。但她在愛荷華州怎麼會找到鰻魚呢？

「如果他們當時沒有發現，現在也不會發現了。那些空有其表的警隊電腦，遠遠比不上美國人的傳統智慧。」

我想我應該要更加心存感激才對，因為其他人的母親可不會像我媽媽般為子女著想吧？

媽媽把收音機音量調低，我才聽見有些聲音從地板那邊傳上來——尖叫聲。前女朋友的尖叫聲；以前最好朋友痛苦的咆

My ex–best friend's wails of pain. The chorus of cries of my ex–friends. The high–pitched squealing of the pigs. I look to mother, who just shrugs. We live in the rural heart of the country, so it's not like anyone will hear them. "Don't worry. I'll give them exactly what they deserve. Nobody hurts my boy."

"Thanks, mother." I say, before taking another bite of pie. While I could have done this myself, mother wanted to do it for me.

And I know what happens when you say no to mother.

哮聲；前朋友們的哭泣合奏聲；豬群尖銳刺耳的哀號聲。我望向媽媽，她聳聳肩。我們住在農村，所以沒有人會聽見他們的聲音。「不用擔心，他們應得的報應，我都會奉還給他們。沒有人可以傷害我的兒子。」

「媽媽，謝謝你。」說罷又再多吃一口餡餅。雖然我可以親自下手，但媽媽想為我做些事，所以就讓她做吧。

況且我很清楚拒絕她會有甚麼後果。

I Did All I Could

Clay and I have never had a great relationship. I tried, but even as an infant he seemed to prefer everyone but me. My husband stayed home with him, they seemed to bond and I was left with a lackluster relationship with my only child. Hugh was great, backed me up on decisions or punishments for Clay. It wasn't his fault.

Clay was a wonderful kid – straight A's all the way through school, lots of volunteer work in high school, he had lots of friends. We just seemed to have incompatible personalities, no matter how much I loved him. There was always something I just couldn't put my finger on, something that kept us distant.

I tried to bond with him, but it never would pan out. It was like we were separate when we were together, like two strangers stuck on a bus. The only times we really enjoyed together were the trips to my friend Karen's lake house. She rarely used it, since it was just her and her husband. We mostly fished while there but never had that "moment" I'd always dreamt of. Clay was noticeably happier there, though. It wasn't much, but it was something.

When he went away to college I knew that any chance we had at a close relationship was gone, but he knew that I loved him, so that had to be enough. Clay lived states away now, and with Hugh long passed he and I had fallen out of touch.

我已竭盡所能

我和 Clay 的關係從來也不好,我很努力維繫,但從幼兒時期開始,他就不再親近我了。以前我丈夫會留在家照顧他,所以他們的關係好像也不錯,而我和這唯一孩子的關係卻沒有一點曙光。Hugh 很好,每次都會替我作決定,又會適當地懲罰 Clay,所以這不是他的錯。

Clay 是個很出色的孩子,學生生涯裏全部科目都考獲甲級成績,中學時參與過很多義工服務,結識了很多朋友。無論我有多愛他,我們怎樣也是合不來的。好像總是有些說不出的東西令到我們水火不容。

我試著與他培養感情,但每當我和 Clay 走在一起時,總是像兩個不相識的人在巴士上同行般,形同陌路。有一次我們到了我朋友 Karan 的湖邊小屋度假,那次是難得大家都享受的時光。不過因為 Karen 和她丈夫沒有孩子,所以很少來這間小屋遊玩。我們大部分時間都在釣魚,雖然我夢寐以求的畫面沒有出現,不過那時候的 Clay 明顯比平常開心一點,雖然不是很誇張,但還是看得出來有差別。

當他上大學後,我就知道我們的關係再也無法變好了,但只要他知道我愛他,我就心滿意足了。Clay 現在搬到很遠的州份了,但自從 Hugh 不在了之後,我們愈來愈少接觸,只會

Just a call on occasion, maybe holidays.

You will never know true despair and helplessness until you see your child's face on the news, with the words, "Missing" plastered over it. Apparently, he and a coworker were last seen sharing their cigarette break and just never came back.

I had to find my son. I prayed for my motherly instincts to kick in. Like a bolt of lightning, I remembered something from one of our brief phone calls, just a tidbit from a story about work Clay had thought I would find interesting, and I suddenly understood. I started driving, taking the same old route. I parked my car down the hill and walked up, slipping in through the back door. I grabbed what I needed, then I opened the basement door and sauntered downstairs like I belonged there.

He looked exhausted, covered in sweat and spattered with blood. "Mother? How did you find me?"

"You're my baby. I'll always find you."
"Do you think you'll get us out of here?"

I nodded and pulled out the pistol I'd snatched from the gun case upstairs.

間中通個電話，大時大節寒暄幾句而已。

真正使我感到絕望無助的，是在新聞上看見兒子的照片，上面大字寫著「失蹤」兩字。據説他和同事小休時出去抽根煙後，就沒有再回來了。

我一定要把兒子找回來！我祈求上天讓我發揮母性本能，助我找回兒子。我突然晴天霹靂，想起 Clay 和我通電話時，他覺得我會感興趣，於是説過一個有關工作的趣聞給我聽。我現在恍然大悟了。我馬上駕車出去，沿著舊路前進。我把車子泊在山下，然後徒步走上山，從後門悄悄溜進去。我拿了所需的東西，接著打開地下室的門，像是回到自己家中般，悠然自得地走下樓梯。

大汗淋漓的他看起來累透了，還有些血跡濺到他的身上。
「媽媽？你怎樣找到我的？」

「你是我的寶貝兒子嘛，我一定會找到你的。」
「你要帶我走嗎？」

我點點頭，抽出了手槍，那是我剛剛在樓上槍盒裏的拿到的。

He looked horrifically angry. I realized suddenly that I'd never seen him angry before. The woman he had tied up and brutalized squirmed and screamed from behind her gag.

"Really? Your own son?" He spat at me.
"I'm your mother, I have to."

"Fuck you."
"I love you, too," I said, and planted a bullet between his eyes.

他勃然大怒，我才突然發現原來我還未看過他生氣的模樣。

那個被他綁起來、凌虐過的女子雖然被堵著嘴巴，但仍失聲尖叫著，並不斷扭動著身體。

「真的假的？我是你的親生兒子啊？」

「我是你的母親，我必須這樣做。」

「去你的！」

「我也愛你。」說罷，我便讓子彈穿越他兩眼之間。

I'm a Very Good Husband

I pulled the thin chain that hung above the floor. The flickering bulb barely lit the area around where I was standing. The basement was filthy with years of neglect but the area underneath his feet was wiped nearly clean.

I've long since stopped flinching every time he yanks and strains against the ropes binding him to the chair in front of me. After all this time, I'm surprised he's still trying to free himself. The first signs of bed sores peek out from underneath his bare thighs and he's covered in his own vomit. I can only assume the wet stench of rot got the better of him. I don't even notice it anymore. Honestly, I've lost track of how long I've had him down here.

I slide the burlap sack off his face. It's soaked with his spit and sweat. He's not yelling this time. No screams for freedom. No curses at me to let him go. No pathetic begging. Just acceptance. There's an anticipation in his eyes. Surrounded by swollen, gray lids, they beckon his eventual end; his death that I will keep at bay for as long as possible. I cannot let myself get all emotional about this. Death would be too favorable an outcome.

廿四孝丈夫

我拉了拉那條懸垂在地板上的細鐵鏈。那顆忽明忽暗的燈泡勉強照亮著我現在站的位置。地牢到處因為多年沒有人打理,髒亂不堪,但他腳下的範圍卻擦得很乾淨。

他每一次都在我面前猛拽猛扯,想要鬆開那條把他綁在椅子上的繩子,但我早已不再畏縮了。不過我很佩服他過了那麼久,還在嘗試為自己鬆綁。在他光脫脫的大腿下方開始長出了褥瘡,然而他現在全身都是自己的嘔吐物。我猜他已經吸光了那股噁心的酸臭味吧?因為我現在沒有嗅到任何味道了呢!老實說,我已經記不起我把他關在這裏有多久了。

我把他頭上的麻布袋拿了下來,那個麻布袋已經浸滿了他的口水和汗水。他這次沒有大吵大鬧,沒有尖叫說想要自由,沒有用髒話來求我放走他,沒有哀求乞討。只是默默地接受了。在他腫得一塊紅一塊灰的眼睛裏,我看見了他命運的結局。但他堅定的眼神告訴我,他仍然抱有一絲盼望。我會盡量把他的死期拖長。我不能為此變得感情用事,殺死他簡直是便宜了他。

He doesn't even look at me anymore. His eyes only stare to the opposite edge of the light where another person sits, covered in a fine, white sheet. I was worried he finally stopped caring about his situation until I took a couple steps toward the other chair. He winced, averting his stare to the more comfortable darkness everywhere else.

"Please," he said. "I know you're not letting me go. Just kill me."

"Then I'd have to worry about hiding your body." I replied, grabbing the sheet and giving it a pull.

"What do you want from me?" He asked pathetically.

"You, of all people, should understand what I'm doing." I said, having fully uncovered my wife's corpse. The bruises on her face and surrounding her neck frozen in the perpetuity of death.

"I'm sorry–" *There's the begging I'm used to.*

"You don't **get** to be sorry." I said like a well-known fact.

He began to cry. A weak attempt to garner my sympathetic side. That's a piece of my personality I learned to hide away only a day after I caught him. You always hear how serial killers are so charismatic and I refused to let him manipulate my humanity. I refuse to feel anything but vindication.

他現在連看也不看我了，只凝望著有光的對面，那裏有個被白色床單蓋著的另一人。我很擔心他已經不再在乎自己的處境了，於是我向另外那張椅子走了幾步，他皺起眉頭，把視線移到其他沒有光的地方。

「拜託了，」他說：「我知道你不會放走我的，殺了我吧。」
「那我不就要處理你的屍體了嗎？」我一邊回答，一邊把床單抓住，一手拉走了它。

「你到底想我怎樣？」他悲淒地問道。
「其他人或許不知道，但你應該很清楚我在幹甚麼吧？」我說道。現在我妻子的屍體大刺刺地展現在我們的眼前。她臉上和頸上佈滿了的瘀傷，因她的死亡而變成永恆的烙印。

「我很抱歉……」這樣的乞求我已經聽了很多遍。
「你不用感到抱歉。」我把這話說得像是件理所當然的事實。

他哭了起來，這顯然為了博取我的同情，而作出的一個弱勢舉動。但從我抓到他的那天起，我就已經收起了自己的同情心。常聽說那些連環殺人犯大多有著超凡的魅力，會讓你乖乖服從，所以我不能讓他操縱我的心。除非有東西證明到他是清白的，否則我都不會有任何反應。

"How many more would you have killed, John?" I asked him, lightly feathering my wife's wiry hair. "If I hadn't walked in on you, how many more wives would've ended up like my own?"

"Just kill me." he whimpered.

"Oh, you will die, John." I tried to sound comforting, "but not until you atone for the fourteen that came before her."

I grabbed my sledgehammer and spread his toes on the floor in front of me.

「你還想多殺多少人啊，John？」我輕撫著太太的如鐵絲般的頭髮問道。「如果那天我沒有識破你，你還想讓多少個女人落得像我太太般的田地？」

「殺了我吧……」他嗚咽著說。

「噢，John，你會死的。」我嘗試用溫和的聲線安撫他：「但你首先要償還了在我太太遇害前，那十四個冤魂的孽債才能死啊。」

我拿起大鎚，然後把他的腳趾攤平在地板上……

Not the Worst Way to Die

"Mommy, what's the worst way to die you can think of?"
Kiera's mother looked surprisedly at her 6 year old daughter.
"Goodness, Kiera! What a question!"

"But what way, Mommy?"
"Oh—I guess a fire would be pretty bad. A house fire, where
you couldn't get out. Why? Mommy's busy, honey...."

"I just wondered," the child answered, and skipped into the
living room.

"Daddy, what's the worst way to die you can think of?"
"Hmmm—car crash? Grizzly bear attack? Daddy's trying
to watch the game, sweetie..., " her father answered absent-
mindedly.

"Oh. OK. I just wondered, " Keira gave a little smile.

She felt much better now. She skipped down the hall, to her
room.

Her parakeet was barely moving now, laying in the bottom
of the little jar she'd closed him in that morning. Probably he
would die very soon, with no air in the jar, but at least nobody
thought that was the worst way to die.

不算最慘的死法

「媽媽，你覺得怎樣才算最慘的死法呢？」

Kiera 的母親一臉茫然地望著自己六歲的女兒，驚訝說道：
「天啊！Kiera，這是甚麼爛問題啊？」

「可是媽媽，那會是怎樣啊？」
「呃……我想被火燒死應該挺慘的吧。例如家居火災吧，被困家中而不能逃脫。你問來幹甚麼呢？親愛的，媽媽正忙著呢……」

「我只是好奇啊。」女孩說罷就跑跳著走到客廳。

「爸爸，你覺得怎樣才算最慘的死法呢？」
「唔……撞車？被大灰熊襲擊？甜心，爸爸正在看球賽，很緊張呢……」Kiera 的父親心不在焉的答道。

「噢，好吧，我只是好奇啊。」Keira 笑了一下。

她現在感覺好很多了，然後在走廊跑跳著，步向自己的房間。

那隻長尾小鸚鵡現在幾乎不動了，今早 Keira 把牠關在玻璃瓶裏，現在牠只是靜靜的躺在瓶底。瓶子裏沒有空氣，牠應該捱不了多久，但至少沒有人認為這樣算是最慘的死法。

She glanced at the empty fishbowl on her dresser—just last week, she'd poured rubbing alcohol into it, and watched her two goldfish loll dizzily about, till they finally floated on top.

Fascinating.

And not the worst way to die.

The Daddy Longlegs in the yard had been fun, too—so satisfying to pull their legs off one by one, till there was nothing left but a useless little body, helplessly skittering in circles in the dirt....but not the worst way to die...

Kiera did feel better now, creeping into her baby sister's room with a plastic bag. She would be an only child again very soon....

And her baby sister?

Well, it wasn't the worst way to die....

她向梳妝台上那空的魚缸瞥了一眼，想起了上個禮拜的事：她把消毒用酒精倒了進去，觀賞著那兩條金魚歪七豎八的游來游去，到最後浮上水面。

真是引人入勝。

但這也不算最慘的死法。

那些在院子裏的長腳蚊也很好玩呢！把牠們的腳逐條逐條剝下來，直到牠們只剩下那副細小但無用的身軀，望著牠們在泥濘裏蹦跳著的無助模樣，真的很治癒啊！但這也不算最慘的死法。

Kiera 現在感覺真的好很多了。拿著塑膠袋的她悄悄潛進妹妹的房間，很快 Kiera 就可以重新當回獨生女了⋯⋯

至於她的妹妹？

嗯，那樣也不算最慘的死法啊⋯⋯

gluttonygreedslothlustprideenvy
WRATH

"Your father has a hard time controlling his anger," my mother would say as she held ice to her bloody lip. "We have to be patient for him. He needs us."

She taught me never to lie. But she was lying when she told the doctor that she'd tripped on a shoe and fell down the stairs. After the doctor left the hospital room, I asked her why she didn't tell the truth.

She looked very sad as she squeezed my hand. "Your father needs us to be there for him. He can't control his anger like most people can. So I lied, which is a *little* bad thing, so that he didn't get in trouble, which would be a *big* bad thing. Do you understand, Sweetie?"

She tried to smile, but it hurt her face.

So here's the thing.

She repeated that line more times than I could count.

And after many years, I *did* understand. I understood very well.

Being unable to control your anger is a *very, very bad* thing.

七宗罪之憤怒

「你父親在控制憤怒方面有困難，」母親邊用冰敷著流血的嘴唇邊說著：「我們要耐心對待他，他很需要我們。」

她教我不要說謊，但她卻跟醫生說謊，說她被鞋子絆倒了，然後摔了下樓梯。醫生離開了病房後，我問她為甚麼不將真相說出來。

她用力捉住我的手，看起來很傷心。「你父親需要我們在身邊支持他，他跟大部分人不一樣，他不能控制自己的憤怒。所以我說謊了，這是件小壞事，讓他不會惹到麻煩，不然那就會是件大壞事了。親愛的，你明白嗎？」

母親想擠出笑容，但這使她的臉很痛。

事情是這樣的。

她重複這句話的次數簡直多不勝數。

多年後，我明白箇中意思了，*真的*清楚明白了。

不能控制憤怒真的是一件*很壞很壞*的事。

It's why Mom ended up in a coma. It's the reason the doctors say she might not wake up.

Now, with the repeated lessons of a lifetime behind me, there are two things that I am absolutely certain of.

The first is that Dad will never be unable to control his anger again. I reflect on this as I finish placing the dirt over a person–sized hole in the ground.

The second is that I will never, ever have a hard time controlling my anger.

Because when I choose to use it, I can control the direction of my **anger** just fine.

媽媽更因此陷入了昏迷狀態，醫生説她可能不會再醒來。

事到如今，長久以來的「生命課堂」教會了我兩件事。

第一件事是在我把泥土翻到那個成人大小的坑洞時，我就知道，控制憤怒對爸爸來説再也不是難事。

第二件事是我永遠都不會在控制憤怒方面有困難。

因為當我要發洩怒氣的時候，我可以處理得很好。

It's Common for People to Undergo a Personality Change after Brain Trauma

"Not the best way to go, is it?"

I looked up to see a guy dressed entirely in black, lounging by a tree. He was scratching his back with a large, simple looking scythe, and his eyes were a deep crimson.

"Are you... the Devil?" I asked, disconcerted.
"The what? Come on," he chortled. "I'm Death. Nice to meet you."
"I'm... dead?"

My eyes went back to the ground– and for the first time I realized that we were in midair. Below us was a car wreck, and a mangled body was leaning out the window. I recognized the watch that had survived the crash: it was the Rolex my dad had given me for my eighteenth birthday. It continued operating, uncaring of the events that transpired as it ticked the time away.

Death shrugged. "I don't know about that. Do you want to live?"
"What?! Aren't you here to take me to the afterlife?!"

He laughed again. "You have a choice. You can go back into your body and continue your life as a cripple, suffering the occasional fit. I understand you have a family to care for, and

腦外傷後人格劇變的現象很普遍

「這不是最理想的死法喔，對吧？」

我抬起頭，望見一個男子倚著樹幹，全身上下都穿了黑色的衣物。有著血紅眼睛的他，用一把巨大、造型簡潔的鐮刀撓著背。

「你是……惡魔嗎？」我驚惶失措地問。
「甚麼？拜託啦！」他咯咯地笑了起來，「我是死神，很高興認識你。」
「我……死了？」

我重新望向地下，才發現原來自己和死神都在半空之中。我們下方有一輛汽車殘骸，還有半個血肉模糊的身軀晾到車窗外。我認得那隻完好無缺的手錶——那隻勞力士手錶是我十八歲生日時，爸爸送給我的禮物。它還在運作，彷彿世事與它毫不相干，仍然滴答滴答地跟隨時間流逝。

死神聳了聳肩，「我不知道啊，你想活下去嗎？」
「啥？你不是要把我帶到極樂世界嗎？」

他又笑了起來，「你有選擇權啊，你可以回到自己的身體繼續生活，不過你將會是個間中痙攣發作的跛子。我知道你還有家人要照顧，如果你死掉的話，他們應該會很懊惱吧。你

they'd be quite distraught with your passing. You shouldn't have drank that last shot of whisky."

Death paused for just a second, and a curious emotion gleamed in his red eyes. "If you want to live, all you need to do is lie back down in your body. If you want to come with me, take my hand."

I looked at his outstretched arm and sighed. I had always told myself I'd rather be dead than crippled. It would be financially responsible for my family as well, who weren't that well off. As his fingers closed around mine, a movement below caught my eye.

My body was moving. A hand trembled, then I was looking down at my own face staring back up at me. My body winked and grinned before squirming its way out of the wreckage.

"What's going on?" I demanded. "I said I didn't want to live as a cripple!"
"You didn't," said Death. "But someone else didn't mind."

不應該連最後那杯威士忌也喝掉的。」

死神頓了一頓，他的血紅眼睛閃過一瞬詭譎的眼神。「如果你想活下去，你只需躺回自己的身體就可以了；如果你想跟我走的話，就抓住我的手吧。」

我望著他伸出的手臂嘆了口氣。我以往經常在想，我寧願死，也不要當跛子。我們不是大富人家，如果我跛了只會加劇家人的經濟負擔。正當死神的手指逐漸靠近我的手時，下方的舉動引起了我的注意。

我的身體在動！我嚇得手都顫抖了，那個「我」正抬頭望著我。「我」眨了眨眼，咧嘴笑著，然後扭動著身體，嘗試從汽車殘骸中離開。

「這到底是怎麼回事？」我問道，「我說過我不想當跛子的啊！！！」
「我知道你不想，」死神說：「但也有其他人不介意喔。」

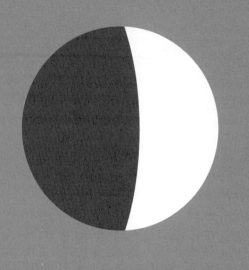

Ruthless Betrayal

無 情 背 叛

At Least We Have Each Other

"Don't worry, Frank. They can't get in. If they try, I'll shoot to kill."

Stanley and Frank had been locked up inside their country house for months, ever since the outbreak started. At first it was safe to go outside. People didn't start manifesting symptoms of such a strange infection until the year before. Experts thought this had been limited to a few, the poor, those in third–world countries without access to civilized medical care.

But the world took notice when it spread to Hollywood and into various national governments.

There was no stopping it. It appeared no one who had been bitten by the soulless wanderers with rotting flesh were immune. Stanley had never missed an episode of "The Walking Dead" and had often joked with friends about what he'd do if there ever was a Zombie Apocalypse.

Now his jokes had become reality.

Stanley had always been a cautious man, one privy to stockpiling food and water, along with weapons and ammunition. He was glad now he had done this. He and Frank were safe and would never run out of water. His large

相依為命

「放心吧，Frank，他們進不來的，如果他們嘗試闖進來，我就把他們射死！」

自從疫情爆發後，Stanley 和 Frank 把自己反鎖在鄉間別墅已經好幾個月了。最初外面還是安全的，那時人們還未出現感染的徵狀，直至上一年，情況開始變得不同了。專家當時認為，疫症只限在一些貧困地區及缺乏醫療保健的第三世界國家出現。

但當它開始蔓延至荷里活及各國政府後，人們才開始正視這個問題。

疫情一發不可收拾，被那些身體腐爛、失去靈魂的怪物咬傷的人，全部無一倖免。那齣以喪屍為題的電視劇《行屍》，Stanley 每集也有看，還經常跟朋友笑說如果真的有喪屍災難的時候他會怎麼做。

現在他的笑話成真了。

Stanley 向來是個謹慎的人，他將廁所當作儲藏室，把食物、水、武器、彈藥都放在裏面。他很慶幸自己做了這些準備功夫，使他和 Frank 安全活下來，也全靠別墅裏那個又大又不受污染的水井，使他們有源源不絕的乾淨水。

and uncontaminated country well gave them that security. The conundrum now was they had run out of food five days ago.

Frank gave his friend a helpless look.

"Now don't panic," Stanley said. "We'll think of something."

He wanted to believe his own words, but the fact remained leaving the house was no longer an option, even at night. Too many infected roamed around as far as the eye could see, and they possessed an unparalleled tenacity and desire to feed.

"At least we have each other," Stanley said and smiled as his stomach rumbled.

No response.

He could hear snarling and growling from outside. Adrenaline surged through Stanley's blood as he grabbed the shotgun, then locked and loaded. They were close. Too close. Stanley turned his back to secure the front door, unaware that Frank catapulted toward him with a sudden leap. Both fell to the floor.

"No, Frank! What are you doing?" Stanley yelled out but was

但現在他們正陷入困境，他們已經斷了糧五天。

Frank 擺出一副無助的表情。

「不用怕，」Stanley 說：「我們會想到辦法的。」

Stanley 也想相信自己的話，但他清楚知道就算是晚上，也不可以離開房子。外面太多受感染的人在附近，他們全部都著了魔，擁有無與倫比的韌性，以及對食物有著極大的渴求。

「我們至少還有彼此……」說罷 Stanley 的肚子便咕嚕地響了起來，他笑了。

沒有回應。

他聽見外面傳來了低吼聲，Stanley 體內的腎上腺素立刻飆升，他馬上拿起獵槍，將子彈上膛。他們很接近，太接近了。

Stanley 轉身走向前門守候，殊不知在他身後的 Frank 突然向他跑過來，一躍而起，撞倒了 Stanley，雙雙倒在地上。

「不！Frank！你在幹甚麼？」Stanley 叫喊道。但他的好朋友現正壓在他身上，使他動彈不得。

no match for his dear friend who now had him pinned down under his weight and was lying on top of him.

And the struggle was on.

Frank wasted no time as he set his sites on Stanley's jugular vein and sank in his teeth. The only noise in the room was Stanley's painful and life–fleeting screams. Within minutes, he stopped struggling, and a pool of blood collected on the floor next to him.

The problem of no food had been solved for the moment.

Frank jumped off of Stanley and took a few steps back, sat down and licked his chops. He panted, aware that he could take his time consuming his new food source and still had plenty of water available for the time being.

And his tail wagged.

他們開始扭打起來。

Frank 分秒必爭地張開嘴巴，向 Stanley 的頸靜脈猛然咬下去。房子內只剩 Stanley 痛苦、奄奄一息的慘叫聲。不出幾分鐘，他沒有再掙扎，而他旁邊的地上出現了一大灘血跡。

斷糧這個問題暫時解決了。

Frank 從 Stanley 的身上跳下來，後退了幾步，然後坐下來舔著嘴。他喘著氣，意識到他有很多時間慢慢享受新的食物，還有源源不絕的水可以讓他暫時活下去。

然後牠擺了擺尾巴。

Caught in Traffic

This was Leslie's hell. Four weeks– or had it been five?– of her being passed from pervert to pervert. They used her like a doll and stripped her of her innocence and virginity. She'd run away from home, and the seemingly charming guy at the coffee shop was actually a human trafficker. Young girls like her made it too easy for guys like him.

The setting of the restaurant for the underground–type customers was comfortably lavish, but Leslie was hardly comfortable standing on the stage in the corner with other terrified girls in minimal clothing waiting to be auctioned. Leslie, despite her predicament, remained arrogantly defiant, resisting her owners and ending in failure every time. Thus, tonight was her third auction.

A furious competition ensued between some fat old guy and a masked man. 20,000 from the Fatty. 20,500 from Masky. It went back and forth, the two furiously raising their signs until the fat man conceded, and she was bought for 150,000. Her only relief was that she wouldn't end up flattened into some semen–stained mattress.

She observed with wary eyes as the man finished dining. What sort of things was he into? After all, it seemed anyone willing to *buy* a human must have a kink or two. As he stood up, he made eye contact with her in anticipation. Perhaps it

少女拍賣會

這對 Leslie 來說是個煉獄。她被一個又一個變態「傳閱」了已經不知四個還是五個星期了。他們對待 Leslie 就像個洋娃娃般，不斷踐踏著她的純真貞潔。那時候她離家出走，在咖啡店遇上了一個看起來很有魅力的男子，豈料他原來是個人販子。對他來說，要讓像 Leslie 這種少女上當，根本不費吹灰之力。

這個專門為黑市交易而設的餐廳，深受一眾見不得光的顧客喜愛。Leslie 現在跟其他嚇壞了、衣著暴露的女孩們一起站在台上的角落，等待著被拍賣掉，使她渾身不自在。雖然身陷窘境，但 Leslie 依然故我，傲慢無禮，又反抗她的主人，使她每次都被退回。所以今晚已經是她第三次被拍賣了。

台下展開了一場激烈的爭奪戰，是一個又老又胖的男子和另一個面具男在競投。胖子叫價兩萬，面具男叫價兩萬零五百。兩個男子就這樣來來回回舉著牌子，最後因胖子放棄競投，面具男以十五萬投得 Leslie。唯一讓她可以放心的地方，就是她不用再躺在那「精」漬斑斑的床褥上了。

待那個男人用餐完畢後，Leslie 謹慎地觀察著他，心裏暗忖著他這人會有甚麼癖好呢？畢竟肯花錢買個人類回來的人，或多或少都會有些怪癖吧。面具男站起來時主動望著她。但不知道是因為當下的環境影響、暴露的衣著，還是因為面具

was the circumstances, or the skimpy clothing, or the soulless expression of the mask, but Leslie found herself shivering.

Ten minutes later, she found herself in the backseat of an expensive–looking car. She'd mentally prepared for things to happen that night, but she'd be damned if she was just going to let it happen. The man slipped off the face covering and placed it in the passenger's seat, and turned around to face her. "Are you okay, miss?"

"As if you care," she growled through gritted teeth.

"As a matter of fact, I find myself very concerned for your well–being." In spite of herself, Leslie's face heated up. The man, though in his early thirties, was fairly handsome without the mask on.

He sighed and started the engine, driving them through the dim–lit slums. "Look, your parents hired me to find you. They've been very worried about you since you left, and you got yourself involved with horrible people."

She recalled the fight that had driven her to flee to the unforgiving streets. Regrettable things had been said by both sides. "Yeah, right."

所展露的冷漠無情所致，Leslie 不住地發抖。

十分鐘後，她已經坐在一輛名貴汽車的後座上。她對於接下來有可能發生的事已經做好了心理準備，但如果她不阻止那些事發生的話，她就真的是活該了。那個男人把面具拿下來，放到乘客座位上，然後轉身面向 Leslie，對她說：「小姐，你還好嗎？」

「你會在乎嗎？」她咬牙切齒地咆哮著。

「但事實上，我真的很關心你過得好不好。」聽到這裏，Leslie 的雙頰不由地發熱了起來。那個男人雖然已經年過三十，但脫下了面具的他，原來長著一副俊臉。

他嘆了口氣，然後啟動了引擎，駛過昏暗的貧民區。「聽好了，你父母聘請了我來找你，在你離家出走之後，他們一直都很擔心你，但你卻遇上了一群可怕的壞蛋。」

她回想起那天令她奪門而出的吵架，還有雙方那些不可挽回的悔氣說話。她只淡淡回應說：「嗯，是的。」

"Frank and Alyssa Reilly, right?"

Leslie perked up at the names.

"There's no way you're really bringing me home."

The man chuckled. "I'd call you intuitive for that comment, but that was sarcasm, right? It's the truth though."

Leslie's features wrinkled in confusion. "Um, what?"

"Your parents will hold a funeral once they give up hope. It really is a shame I couldn't find you." The car was on the freeway now, speeding too fast for her to abandon the vehicle.

"But it wouldn't be your first time in a **basement**, would it?"

「Frank Reilly 和 Alyssa Reilly，對吧？」

Leslie 聽見熟悉的名字，精神抖擻起來。

「你不會真的帶我回家的，對嗎？」

那個男人笑了起來，「你說這句話是出於直覺嗎？還是在諷刺我？不過你說得沒錯喔。」

Leslie 不解地皺著眉頭問道：「嗯？甚麼？」

「當你父母絕望得放棄尋回你的時候，他們就會舉辦葬禮了。我找不到你真是太可惜了呢！」車子正在高速公路上奔馳，使 Leslie 無法跳車逃走。

「我想你對**地牢**生活已經不陌生了，對嗎？」

Katie

Hello, Mum.

First off, I'm sorry for not being the daughter you always wanted me to be. I never had good grades, never was very polite, and generally was disliked by the older generation. The caning didn't do much, to be honest. I just yelled so you would stop.

I'm sorry about the time I broke your phone when you confiscated mine. There's a few hundred dollars inside my bank, you can withdraw all of it; I won't be touching that again. See, I'm... let's just say eloping. With Mark.

When you shouted at me last night, about how ashamed you were of me for switching boyfriends like a cheap slut, I realized that you were right, and that I was the type of daughter no mother wanted to have. But you're wrong about Mark; I've only known him a week, but he's an absolute gem.

Maybe I'll contact you sometime in the distant future after we're married, just to show you how wrong you were about him. Until then, please stay healthy and well, and be happier knowing I'm out of your life.

Love,
Katie.

私奔

親愛的媽媽：

我想先跟你道歉，我沒有成為你心目中理想的女兒，對不起。我在學校不曾名列前茅，又很沒禮貌，長輩通常也不喜歡我。不過說實話，你用藤條打我其實沒多大作用，我大叫只是想你停手而已。

那次你沒收了我的電話，我為了出氣，也把你的電話弄壞了，對不起。我銀行戶口裏有幾千元，你全部提出來吧，我不會再用了。呃……我要跟 Mark……私奔。

昨晚你罵我讓你很丟臉，說我換男朋友的頻密程度像個低俗的婊子。你說得很對，看我這副德性，任何媽媽也會嫌棄吧。但你看錯了 Mark，雖然我認識他只有一個星期，但他真的是個難能可貴的好男人。

如果我們將來結婚了，我會再聯絡你的，我要證明你看錯了他。在沒有我的日子，請好好保重，也要過得比以前更愉快。

愛你的 Katie 上

The note that was now in her family's mailbox replayed itself in her mind again, and she just sat there, numb.

Physically numb.

The ropes were cutting into her wrists and ankles.

這封信現在靜靜地躺在她家信箱，而她就坐在那裏，沒知覺地回想起信的內容。

名副其實的失去了知覺。

那些繩子正逐漸陷進她的手腕和腳踝……

I Love My Wife

I pressed my wife's sleeping body closer to mine, armed wrapped around her. I remember when we first met, that brisk August morning, waiting in line for coffee. I made her laugh and we sat and talked for what seemed like hours, it was wonderful. I've loved her since that day.

With a heavy sigh I opened my eyes and expelled the memories. Rising from the bed I looked around our squalid bedroom, containing nothing more than walls, a water stained ceiling, and our bed. There was so much I wish I could do for her, so much she deserved, that I just couldn't give to her. With a sigh, I crept out of the room and walked onto the balcony.

I removed a receipt for a life insurance policy from my pocket and milled it over. Perhaps tonight I would make good on it. But the city was beautiful tonight. Too beautiful. I couldn't die on a night like this. Maybe I'd jump tomorrow. Or maybe the day after that. When you think about killing yourself it seems so easy, but actually doing the deed is so much harder.
As I stood at the edge I felt a surge of pressure on my back, shoving me over the railing. Frantically I reached out to grab the edge of balcony, hooking three fingers onto it. Before I could call my wife for help up I glanced up to see her already on the balcony. I shot her a thankful smile. A sinister grin drew across her face as her shoe dug into my fingers.

愛妻心切

我輕輕靠近妻子熟睡的身軀，伸手環抱著她，回想起我們最初相識的情景。當時是八月，在一個朝氣勃勃的早上，我們一起排著隊買咖啡。我逗得她笑了，我們就這樣坐在咖啡店聊了好幾個小時。那時候真的很美好，從那天起我便深愛著她。

我長嘆了一口氣，然後張開了眼睛，讓回憶的畫面褪去。我從床上站起來，環顧著我們這間骯髒不堪的睡房，除了四面牆、充滿水漬的天花板，還有我們的床之外，甚麼也沒有。我真的很希望能為心愛的她做些甚麼，她值得更好的，只是我沒有能力……我又嘆了一口氣，然後靜悄悄地溜出房外，走到陽台。

我從口袋拿出一張人壽保險的收據，然後把它撕碎了。或許這晚我能把它兌現了呢。但這晚的城市很美，太美了，我不想在這個美麗的晚上死去，不如明天再跳吧，那不如後天吧？你以為自殺看似很容易嗎？但原來實際執行起來比想像中困難得多。我站在邊緣時，背後有股力量把我推倒在欄杆外面。我拚命地抓著陽台的邊緣，但只有三隻手指抓得到。我正想開口向妻子求救，但我抬頭望到她已經站在陽台，我報以一個感恩的笑容。但她臉上卻展露著陰險的奸笑，一腳踩在我的手指上。

Just for a Moment

"Let me show you this one," Mom said as she rolled up her sleeve with a devious smirk on her face. There was a crudely tattooed crab. "I'm a cancer. When I was little, the laundromat we went to had a fortune telling machine, you put the quarter in where your birthday fell. I didn't know what Gemini was or Aries, nothin' like that but I figured they had to be types of death, because CANCER is a death!" She started to laugh so hard she got caught up coughing on her cigarette smoke.

When she recovered from her coughing fit, she gave me a wink. "I'll show you one of my other favs. See this?"

I nodded. "It's a bird in a cage. Why is it locked up?"

"Well, I reckon I feel like my entire life people have tried to keep me locked up, kept me from being free. People just don't really understand me. They get court orders to make me take meds or... or force me to get treatment, or like when they've taken you away from me. Fuck them, right?"

"Right. But Mom... have you?"
"Have I what?" She exhaled the last bit of smoke into the air of our tiny shack.
"Been taking your meds?"
"Hunny, don't you worry your head 'bout that."

紋身的故事

媽媽捲起袖子，用奸狡的笑容跟我説著：「你看看這個，」
她向我展露著一個畫功粗糙的螃蟹紋身。「我是巨蟹座的。
小時候有間自助洗衣店，裏面有個算命機器，只要在你生日
日期那格投入二十五美分，它就會告訴你運程。我那時還不
懂甚麼叫雙子座，甚麼叫白羊座，但我知道它們是不同名稱
的死法，因為巨蟹座跟癌症的英文一樣是『Cancer』，代表
死亡！」吸著煙的她哈哈大笑，笑得嗆到了煙，咳了起來。

當她回復正常的呼吸節奏後，她向我打了個眼色，「這個是
我最愛的紋身之一，看到嗎？」

我點點頭：「有隻鳥兒在籠子裏，為甚麼鎖著牠呢？」

「唔，我總覺得一生以來人們都想把我鎖起來，剝削我的自
由，他們只是不懂我而已。他們用法院命令來要我吃藥，又
逼我接受治療，甚至要把你帶離我身邊。去他們的！你説對
不對？」

「對啊，但媽媽，你有沒有……？」
「有沒有甚麼？」她呼出最後一口煙，任由它飄散到小棚屋
的空氣之中。
「有沒有吃過藥？」
「親愛的，你不用擔心我啦！」

I could hear a car pull into the driveway. Maybe two.

"But this one is my absolute favorite." She smiled at me as she pointed to her forearm.

"The one that has my name on it?"

"Yes, sweet baby. It is."

Then there was banging on the door.

Mom began to tear up as she pulled out a box cutter.

More banging.

"Open up, we know you have her in there!"

"You don't want to leave me do you? You don't want to go back to the foster home, do you? Leave me behind to be so lonely?"

I shook my head no.

"Child services is here with law enforcement, **OPEN UP!**"

我聽見有車子駛進我們的車道，好像是兩輛車。

「但這個才是我最最愛的一個！」她望著我，笑著指向她前臂的一個紋身。
「有我名字的這個紋身？」
「是的，甜心，沒錯。」

門外傳來了呼呼聲。

媽媽把美工刀拿出來的時候，眼眶都濕了。

那些呼呼聲愈來愈猛烈了。

「開門！我們知道她在你手上！」
「我知道你不想離開我的，對吧？我知道你不想回去那個寄養家庭的，對吧？剩我一人會很寂寞的吧？」

我搖搖頭。

「兒童服務組現正執法，**開門！**」

She began to whisper. "Want me to give you your own type of tattoo, baby? And I'll give myself a matching one." Tears rolled down her cheeks.

"What will it be?"
"A straight line."

"What does it mean?"
"That we have a linear connection to be together forever. It means no one will take you away from me ever again."

"Where will you put it?"
"Right here." She took her index finger and drew an imaginary line down my elbow to my wrist.

"Will it hurt?"
"Just for a moment."

她對我輕聲說：「寶貝，你想要個屬於你、獨一無二的紋身嗎？我也會跟你紋個一樣的，湊成一對。」說罷眼淚便流了下來。

「那會是甚麼圖案呢？」
「一條直線。」

「那代表甚麼？」
「代表著我們會有著永不間斷的聯繫，代表著再沒有人能從我身邊搶走你了。」

「要紋在哪裏？」
「這裏。」她用食指在我的手肘憑空畫了一條線，一直畫到我的手腕。

「會痛嗎？」
「痛一陣子就沒事了。」

Children Should Be Seen and Not Heard

My sister was always the good, quiet one, never speaking unless spoken to, always doing what she was told. I wasn't like that. I spoke my mind, and even when I was silent, I usually showed myself in some way. Sometimes accidents would happen, where I would trip or knock something over. I was always the noisy one.

"Children should be seen and not heard," our mother would snap, sometimes glaring at me through her blue-rimmed glasses, sometimes not looking at all.

One day I went too far. I was walking through the living room and tripped over our mother's computer cord.

"Shit!" I said as I fell down.

I knew something was wrong when our mother didn't say anything. She was silent, looking at me through her blue-rimmed glasses. Then she looked away.

The next day our mother went into the garage and came back with a piece of plywood.

"Do not make a sound," she warned, then swung it at my head.

孩子安靜才乖

姊姊很乖巧、很安靜,除非媽媽要她開聲,否則她都不說話,非常聽話。而我則跟她相反,只要我想說話,我就會說出口,就算我不發出聲音,也會用其他方法表現自己。有時我又會出一些意外,例如會絆倒或是打翻東西。我總是嘈吵的那個。

「孩子安靜才乖。」媽媽會很生氣的跟我說,有時會透過她那藍色框眼鏡瞪著我,有時甚至不會正眼望著我。

有一天我玩得過火了,我穿過客廳時不小心絆到了媽媽的電腦電線。

「媽的!」我跌倒時叫道。

我知道當媽媽默不作聲時,就代表大事不妙了。她沒有開口罵我,而是透過她那藍色框眼鏡瞪著我,然後別過頭去。

第二天媽媽走進去車庫,然後拿著一塊木夾板回來。

「不要作聲。」她警告我,然後把木夾板揮到我的頭上。

When I woke, my face was in pain.

"This will sting a little," my mother said, standing over me holding the black bottle of hydrogen peroxide that she put on our cuts.

She poured, and I tried to stay silent, but it was too much. I moved my tongue to scream, but I couldn't find it, and my mouth was filled with blood. I tried to open my lips but they were sewn together. Frantic, I thrashed my body around, desperately trying to convey some message.

"Be still, child," my mother said. "You'll get the peroxide in your eyes."

當我醒來時，我的臉很痛。

「這個會有一點刺刺的。」站在我旁邊的媽媽説道，手裏拿著一個裝滿雙氧水的黑色瓶子，準備塗在我們的傷口上。

她把雙氧水倒下來，我盡力保持安靜，但真的太痛了。我想尖叫，但舌頭不見了，我嘴裏全都是血！我想張開嘴巴，但雙唇被縫了起來了……我瘋狂扭動著身體，拚命地想要跟媽媽「説話」。

「乖孩子，不要亂動，」媽媽説：「不然雙氧水會跑進眼睛喔。」

My Boyfriend Has a Weird Obsession

I think I might have to get a second job to support my boyfriend's addiction.

We've been going out for six months, and for the most part things have been going well until recently. He's been sneaking around, hiding receipts and not telling me what he's been buying.

I know what you're thinking. He's cheating. Trust me, I suspected that too. But it's not that. I know because yesterday I stumbled onto what he's been up to.

Jake has a candle addiction. I know it's weird, but there you have it. He's been buying two to three large jar candles a week every time he gets paid. Maybe it's none of my business, but considering we just moved in together… well… Hey, a girl's got a right to know! Don't judge!

Anyway, this has been going on for weeks. And the weird thing is he's not buying all the same scent. His choices are random, the weirdest thing. I could understand buying all the same scent, but he brings home citrus, vanilla, sea breeze and stuff like oatmeal cookie scented candles all in one purchase.

I just don't understand it.

男朋友的怪癖

我想我應該要多打一份工，才可以應付男朋友的癖好。

我們在一起已經半年了，在這之前一直都相安無事。但最近他經常神出鬼沒，把購物收據藏起來，又不告訴我他買了些甚麼。

我知道你在想甚麼，他出軌了嘛。相信我吧，我也這樣懷疑過，但他沒有出軌，因為我昨天意外地揭發了他最近一直在幹甚麼。

Jake 對蠟燭上了癮。很奇怪對吧？但事實就是這樣，他一領到薪金就會買蠟燭回來，每個禮拜都會買兩至三瓶大蠟燭回來。本身這真的不關我事，但考慮到我們才剛剛住在一起嘛……呃……大姐我有權知道吧！不要批評我！

怎樣也好，他已經好幾個禮拜也是這樣了。讓我不解的是，他不是總買著同一個味道，更奇怪的是，他的選擇都是隨機的。如果他只買同一個味道的話，我倒是能理解。但他有一次買了柑橘味、雲呢拿味和海洋味回來，還有個聞起來像燕麥曲奇的。

我真的搞不懂。

I also don't understand the sudden candle obsession. Why the need to buy so many? The apartment smells great, but the haze of scented burning wax in strange combinations of smells can get a little overwhelming. And he's been increasing the number he buys per week since last week.

Every room has lit candles now. I'm a hopeless romantic at heart, but this is a little ridiculous. Setting a mood is one thing. Making the house look like you're calling up the dead… Sheesh!

I knew it was time for an intervention.

I walked into our spare bedroom. Jake has more candles in there than anywhere, all different scents. And they weren't working well together at all. The combination of the 50 of them together gave off a pungent odor that caused bile to rise in my throat. I could hardly choke it back to ask Jake what was going on.

He polished a couple of hunting knives he had purchased last month, his old obsession before he had started collecting candles. Then he walked over and locked the door.

我也不懂他為甚麼突然對蠟燭上了癮，買這麼多回來幹甚麼？雖然房子很香，但那些香薰蠟燭的煙霧混和在一起之後，我有點透不過氣來。自上個星期起，他每星期買蠟燭的數量還愈來愈多了。

現在每個房間也點了蠟燭，雖然我心底裏是很喜歡浪漫的，但這樣太荒謬了吧？製造氣氛是一回事，但把房子弄得像要召喚亡靈般就⋯⋯哎！

唔，是時候要阻止他了。

我走進了備用臥室，Jake 在這裏放了最多蠟燭，全部都是不同味道的，同時燒起來就一點也不好聞。五十種不同的香味混和一起，變成了一種刺激的氣味，使我幾乎吐了出來，但我強行忍住不讓自己吐出來，然後找 Jake 問他到底發生甚麼事。

他打磨了幾把獵刀，那些刀是他上個月買的。在還未對蠟燭上癮之前，他最喜歡的就是刀了。他走了過來，然後把門鎖上了。

"What in the world are you doing?"

He smiled and walked to the closet door. "I have a surprise for you."

"Oh?"

He opened the door, and tears pricked my eyes as I choked and gagged, now fully aware where the smell was coming from. It wasn't the candles. It was worse, so much worse.

"I dug up my old girlfriend a few weeks ago," Jake said as he wheeled out a wheelchair containing a corpse. He opened a large black book he had also been keeping in the closet and then grabbed me by the wrist. "I can't live without her, nor can I live without you. I've figured out a way I can have you both."

「你在搞甚麼鬼啊?」

他微笑著走向衣櫃,「我給你準備了驚喜。」

「嗯?」

他打開衣櫃門,我有點呼吸困難,又想作嘔,使我快要哭出來了。然後我才清楚意識到那些氣味從何而來。那些氣味原來不是來自香薰蠟燭,而是來自更糟、更噁心的東西。

「幾個禮拜前我把前女友掘了出來,」Jake 邊說著,邊推著一輛輪椅出來,上面載著一具屍體。他又把另一樣藏在衣櫃很久的東西拿了出來,那是一大本黑色的書。他打開了書,然後抓住我的手腕。「沒有她我活不下去,但沒有你我也活不下去。我找到可以讓你們並存的方法了!」

I'm a Very Good Girl

I always obey my parents. *Don't jump on the furniture, Don't tease the dog, Eat your veggies.*

They always want what's best for me and I try hard to be the best daughter in the world.

Safety first, daddy loved to say. Whether we were going to a playground or riding the bus, he was very focused on keeping mommy and me safe from harm. Years ago, he even taught me to safely shoot his beloved rifle.

I think that's why he moved us out to the country. Our nearest neighbor is on the western horizon and you can only see their chimney when standing on the cliffs behind our house. It's always so nice and quiet out here. Lonely at times, but very comfortable.

It got even lonelier a few weeks ago when Bucky, our two year old Golden Retriever, got real sick and died. I miss him so much. Daddy buried him at the base of the cliffs and I used to visit his grave almost every day. He was just a dog, though. We can always get another one.

I can't as easily get a new mommy.

The last time I saw her was three days ago talking with daddy

我是個乖女兒

我很聽從父母的話。*不要在傢具上跳來跳去；不要故意惹怒狗狗；要吃蔬菜⋯⋯*

他們總是想將最好的東西都給我，而我也很努力去當世上最乖的女兒。

*安全第一。*爸爸常常提醒我們。無論是去遊樂場玩耍，還是坐巴士，他都很注重安全，不讓我和媽媽受傷。很多年前，他更教了我如何使用他心愛的來福槍。

我想這也是他讓我們舉家搬到鄉下地方的原因吧。我們最近的鄰居在西邊，即使我們從屋後的懸崖望過去，也只能看到他們家的煙囪。這裏總是很美好，很安靜。雖然有時會感到寂寞，但住在這裏真的很舒適。

幾個星期前，我們那隻兩歲的金毛尋回犬 Bucky，突然病得很重，然後過世了，我就更寂寞了。我很想念牠。爸爸把他埋在懸崖那邊的泥土下，我幾乎每天也會到牠的墳前拜訪牠。不過牠只是隻狗狗，我們可以再養一隻。

但媽媽就不能再養一個。

我最後一次見到她已經是三天前，當時她和爸爸在後院討論

in the backyard. She got real sick after coming home from her monthly grocery run in the city and she slept for days. I really thought she was getting better until she started coughing up blood and her skin began to look like pea soup. Daddy hasn't let me go in the backyard since then.

There's a fresh mound of dirt next to Bucky's. I miss her so much.

For the last two days, daddy has been sitting at the top of the cliffs, watching and waiting. The groceries mommy brought home will feed me for another month, but after that, I don't know what I'll do.

I used to pass the time by listening to the radio, but lately, all they broadcast are emergency warnings about some deadly virus spreading across country. I hear them use the term "reanimated" a lot. I turned it off yesterday and am too scared to turn it back on.

I can hear daddy's deep cough echoing down the cliff at night. I'm scared to be alone, but I promised him I'll do whatever he tells me as I know he only wants the best for me. So when he said *"Sarah, the only way to make sure I won't hurt you is to shoot me in the head."*, I cried but obeyed.

著甚麼事情。她每個月也會到城裏的超市補充日用品，但那次回來後，她就染上了重病，睡了很多天。我本以為媽媽很快就會好起來，但她開始咳血，皮膚也漸漸變成像豌豆湯那樣黃黃綠綠的。自那時起，爸爸就不再讓我踏足後院。

現在 Bucky 旁邊有一個新挖的坑洞。我很想念她。

最近這兩天爸爸都坐在懸崖邊，看著，等待著。媽媽之前在超市買回來的東西足夠讓我吃一個月，但吃光了之後，我就不知該怎麼辦了。

我以前都是靠聽收音機來打發時間，但最近的廣播全都是緊急警報，說有種致命病毒正在國內擴散。我聽見他們常常提及「活死人」這個詞語。昨天，我把收音機關掉了，再也不敢打開它。

在夜裏，我聽見爸爸激烈的咳嗽聲在峭壁裏迴響著。雖然我很怕只剩自己一個人，但我答應了爸爸，無論他叫我做甚麼我也會照做，因為我知道他只會給我最好的東西。所以當爸爸對我說：「*Sarah，為了確保我不會傷害你，唯一的方法，就是向我的頭一槍轟下去。*」我哭了，但還是乖乖照做了。

The Scarecrow

I stood on the porch of my childhood home, idly swinging my father's hatchet in small arcs and staring out at the acreage he'd toiled over for the better part of 30 years. The sun had set some time ago now, but I remained enthralled by all his life had come to. He'd been a hard working man, and the fruits of his labor could quite literally be plucked from this land.

Before me stood the crop over which my dad had poured his blood, sweat and tears. Corn. Dozens of acres of pristine, beautiful corn. Untouched by the hand of man other than the one which put it into the ground, my father had pulled pure American spirit out of the soil each and every year. It was a thing to behold.

However, I'd always thought that in the darkness, the corn took on a more sinister tone. The absence of light caused the many angles to coalesce into what could easily be mistaken for living things moving around, and the rustling of the plants in the wind seemed to mask a host of more ominous noises.

Then there was the scarecrow. Standing where I was now, on the porch, you could see it straight ahead, staring back at you. The thing had frightened me as a child, but my dad had always insisted it was an important part of the farm, and that I'd understand one day when it was mine.

稻草人

我站在兒時住處的門廊上，一邊小幅度地晃悠著父親那把短柄小斧，一邊凝望著那片他辛苦耕耘三十載的田野，看得入神。月色雖已初現，而我仍樂於浸淫在父親努力一生的成果。他是個很勤奮的人，這片茂盛的土地反映了他所有付出的心力，上面滿是名副其實的收穫。

我面前這些農作物，全部都是父親用血、汗和淚水耕種出來的。在這片面積有幾十英畝的麥田裏，均種滿了新鮮又飽滿的穀物。由插秧到收割，父親都一手包辦，從不假手於人。他年復一年、努力不懈地工作，展現著美國人堅毅的精神，非常值得欣賞。

但有時在夜闌人靜之時，我不禁覺得那些穀物看起來很陰森。在光線不足的環境下，它們的影子交疊時，看起來就像有些生物在到處走動，很容易讓人產生錯覺，而它們被風吹得沙沙作響的時候，又好像是要把一些更詭異的聲音掩蓋掉似的。

還有那個稻草人，如果你站在我身處的門廊位置，你就可以清楚的看見它，而它也會直直的回瞪著你。我小時候常常被他嚇壞，但爸爸每次也會強調稻草人的用處，他還告訴我，當我將來成了農場主時，就會明白它有多重要了。

Now that the day had come, I guess I did really understand why it needed to be there. Disquieting as it sometimes seemed, it did cast a certain watchful eye over the corn. Looked at from that angle, it seemed to be a welcome, ever–present guardian which would look over my harvest for years to come. I stepped off the porch and winded my way down the dirt path toward the small clearing where it stood.

The corn rustled around me, and a chill ran down my spine. Was it just the wind, or was there something out there now, watching me from between the stalks?

The scarecrow loomed closer, and I felt a little safer in its gaze. It was high on a wooden post which had stood in that exact spot since long before I was born, and the weight it now bore was indeed helping to bolster my spirits. There was nothing out there – it was just my imagination.

Reaching the post, I stood before the scarecrow. The hatchet still swung idly by my side, and I gazed up at the form on the beam. The moonlight glinted off of my father's lifeless eyes, and a small smile played itself across my face. I dropped the hatchet at the base of the post, where the blade – now stained a dark shade of red – dug into dirt which was mottled with the same crimson tone. I wouldn't need a weapon anymore – the scarecrow would keep me safe.

而現在我真的成了農場主，我想我終於理解到它為何要站在那裏了。雖然有時候它會讓人很不安，但它確實有牢牢地看顧著麥田，又時刻保持警惕，就此而言，它正是個殷勤又無處不在的守護者，在未來的日子裏仍舊會看守著我的莊稼。我走出門廊，踏上了那條通往稻草人那邊空地的泥路。

那些穀穗在我周圍沙沙作響，使我打了個冷顫。到底是因為有風吹過，還是有甚麼東西正躲在穀物叢裏觀察著我？

我愈來愈靠近那個稻草人了，在它的視線範圍裏下，我感到安心了一點。由我出生開始，它所在的位置就沒有變過，到了現在它還是高高的站在木柱上，身負重任的它使我信心更加堅定。那裏其實甚麼也沒有，一切只是我的幻想。

我走近木柱，站在稻草人面前。我還在晃悠著那把短柄小斧，然後抬頭望著那道光。我望著那道從我父親早已沒有生氣的雙目反映出來的月光，使我臉上露出一絲微笑。我把小斧砍進那條柱子，刀片現在染成了深紅色，呈現著跟泥土一樣的深紅色調。我不再需要武器了，稻草人總是讓我很有安全感。

My Sister's Hogging the Bathroom Again

My sister Amy is hogging the bathroom again. She doesn't do it every night, thank goodness, but....

I don't know how she always manages to figure out which bathroom I'm going to use, and when I'm going to go in there, but she does, and gets in before I do. I hate when she does this.

"Amy?" I ask, timidly. I don't want her to get mad at me. She got really mad once. Now I just wait. "C–can I please get in there?"

I thought she'd stop this when we moved to a house with two bathrooms....

"Erica, honey, who are you talk—oh." My mother comes down the hall. "Again?"
"Yes," I whisper. "Can you make her leave?"

My mother's face is grim and sad, as it usually is nowadays. "Amy? You need to get out of the bathroom, please. Please, honey? I'm s—"

The bathroom door opens. My sister glides out, dripping wet, blue, and bloated. Her tongue lolls out of her mouth, and there's some vomit on her chin, just like there was the day she

姊姊又佔著浴室了

姊姊 Amy 又佔著浴室了。還好她不是每晚也是這樣的，謝天謝地。不過……

她不知怎的，總是知道我想用哪個浴室，但總之每次我想進去的時候，她就會比我早一步在浴室裏出現。我很討厭她這樣。

「Amy？」我膽怯地問道，因為我不想惹她生氣。有一次她氣得瘋了，所以現在我只好默默地等待。「請……請問我可以進來嗎？」

我還以為搬到了這個有兩間浴室的房子之後，就能解決這個問題了……

「親愛的 Erica，你在跟誰說……噢。」媽媽從大廳走過來。「又是這樣？」
「是的，」我低聲説：「你可以請她離開嗎？」

媽媽臉上掛著擔憂又傷心的表情，媽媽最近常常也是這個模樣。「Amy？可以請你快點從浴室裏出來嗎？親愛的，拜託了。我……」

浴室門徐徐打開了，姊姊緩緩地溜出來。她不但滿身濕透，

overdosed and drowned in the bathtub three years ago.

My mother turns away, and I hear a sob—she still blames herself. I try not to cringe away as Amy strokes my cheek—I feel only icy air, but if I cringe, Amy will get mad, and follow me everywhere till I let her touch me without cringing. She glides down the hall, fading as she goes.

I don't know why she does this. I'm scared to ask, in case she gets really mad again.

I'm afraid then she might do more than just hog the bathroom.

Author: Sandi Kennedy 129

而且又藍又浮腫，舌頭垂在嘴邊，下巴還有些嘔吐物。她現在的模樣跟三年前那天，她因為過量服藥，溺死在浴缸裏的遺容一模一樣。

媽媽別過了臉，然後我聽見了飲泣聲，她還在怪責自己。當 Amy 摸摸我的臉時，我盡量不退縮。雖然我只感覺到一股冰冷的空氣，但如果我退縮，Amy 就會很生氣，她會一直跟著我，直到我讓她碰我，而我不退縮為止。然後她就向著大廳溜走，漸漸消失了。

我不知道她為甚麼要這樣做，我不敢問她，生怕又會惹她生氣。

我很害怕如果惹怒了她，她不會只是佔著浴室那麼簡單。

Wretched Dilemma
困 境 抉 擇

The Choice

I opened my eyes.

I found myself in what looked like an old basement. It smelled of decay and damp, and as I pulled myself up from the ground I could see a small candle lit on a table in the center of the room.

As I got to my feet, I could see another item glinting in the soft light, propped up by the table was a shiny new chainsaw. A note on the side read **"Use me to LIVE".**

My head was in agony and I couldn't remember how I'd got there, or even where there was.

A small red light in the corner of the room drew my attention.

A camera.

Whoever had put me down here was watching me right now. I began calling out as loud as I could, hoping that someone would hear me, but after an hour my throat was sore and it had done no good.

Wherever I was seemed to be far away from anyone else.

抉擇

我張開雙眼。

我發現自己身處在一個像老舊地牢的地方，有股腐壞和潮濕的氣味。原本坐在地下的我撐起身來，看到房間的中央放著一張桌子，上面有根點著了的蠟燭。

我站起來之後，才看到桌子上還有另一樣東西在閃耀著。那是一把新簇簇、閃閃發亮的電鋸，旁邊有張紙條寫著：「**用我來活下去**」。

我頭痛得快炸開了，我想不起來我是怎樣來到這裏的，也不知道這裏是甚麼地方。

房間角落的一點紅光引起了我的注意。

攝錄機。

把我抓到這裏的人正監視著我。我盡可能地大聲呼喊，希望有人會聽見我求救。但我喊了一個小時，喊得喉嚨都痛了，完全沒用。

看來這裏附近都沒有人。

I sat down and my stomach growled. How long had it been since I'd eaten anything? I didn't know.

I sat in there for what seemed like days.

Asking for food turned to begging, but still, no one came to provide anything to eat.

Even prisoners got food, I thought. Whoever was keeping me there must be trying to starve me to death.

It was then that I noticed a line had been drawn around the calf muscle of my leg. Dotted lines like on an envelope. and suddenly I realized why I hadn't been fed.

The sick bastard who'd taken me wanted me to cut off my own leg.

Well fuck that, I thought, There's no way I'm going to do that.

But hunger has a way of reducing even the most ethical of people to the extreme.

Another day or two passed. I felt exhausted, so weak. I'd found a spider on the wall and gobbled it up. It was disgusting

我坐下來，肚子打鼓了。距離上一次吃東西有多久了？我不知道。

我就這樣坐在這裏好幾天了。

我之前還會「要求」他們給我食物，現在卻變成了「乞求」，儘管如此，還是仍然沒有人拿食物給我。

我心裏暗忖著，就算囚犯也有東西吃吧，把我關在這裏的那個人肯定想把我活活餓死。

此時我才發現腳上被畫了一條像空郵信封上的虛線，圈著我整條小腿。我才恍然大悟，原來這就是他們不給我食物的原因。

抓我的那個變態想我把自己的腳切下來。

吃屎吧，我絕對不會這樣做的。

但再有道德的人，在飢餓面前都要低頭。

過一天還是兩天，我很累了，也很虛弱。我看到牆上有隻蜘蛛，然後一把將牠吞掉了。雖然牠在我口裏蠕動的感覺非常

and squirmed in my mouth, but it felt so good to finally eat again.

I felt close to death when I finally considered the chainsaw. It would hurt so much, but after I passed out, I'd have some meat to eat, as disgusting as the idea was.

I put the blade to my leg and closed my eyes. When I pressed the button, the sound of the blade cutting was almost worse than the pain. I got through the bone before a cold sensation of shock washed over me and I passed out.

When I awoke, I found myself bandaged up. my stump had been surgically stitched up and a hot pie sat on the table next to the candle. I knew what the meat inside consisted of, but I ate it all just the same.

I smiled. The worst was over. I would survive this. I would find a way.

And then I noticed the dotted line on the other leg...

噁心，但終於有東西下肚的感覺實在是太好了！

我下定決心要用電鋸的那一刻，我才感覺到自己離死亡很近。那肯定很痛，但我昏迷過後就可以有肉吃了，雖然這件事跟那個人的想法一樣噁心。

但我還是把電鋸放了在腳上，然後閉緊眼睛，按下按鈕。鋸齒切割的聲音幾乎跟痛楚一樣使我難受。我把骨頭切開了，一陣冷冽的寒意顫動全身，然後我便昏過去了。

當我醒過來時，已經有人幫我縫好了腿上的傷口，還用繃帶包紮好了。桌子上的蠟燭旁邊放著一個熱烘烘的餡餅，我很清楚裏面的餡是用甚麼造的，但我還是把它吃光光。

我笑了，苦難終於都過去了！我可以捱得過的，我會找到出路的。

然後我看到另一隻腳上有一條新的虛線……

The Worst Thing

The day after my fifteenth birthday, my neighbor, Mr. Colton, came over asking to borrow some sugar. His eyes roved up and down my body as he asked. I thought this was the worst thing.

Before I could give him the sugar, he lunged at me, pressed a cloth over my mouth. When I woke up, I was in the back of a van, bound at the wrists and ankles. I thought this was the worst thing.

I think I'm underground. I don't know how long I've been here. Days, at least. The room I'm in is small and cell–like, with a few spots to hold candles. There is a huge pentagram carved into one wall.

Men and women come and go, bringing me food and taking away food and bringing me a chamber pot and taking it away. Sometimes they forget to bring me food. I thought this was the worst thing.

Once a day I get bread and water. Once, I complained that I was still hungry. They told me I could eat some of the roaches for protein. I thought this was the worst thing.

最糟糕的事

我十五歲生日後那天，鄰居 Colton 先生過來跟我借砂糖。他向我借糖時雙眼不停上下打量著我的身體，我以為這是最糟糕的事。

我還未去拿砂糖給他，他就撲向我，用布掩著我的嘴巴。當我醒過來的時候，我已經身處小貨車的後座，手腳都被綁了起來，我以為這是最糟糕的事。

我想我是在地底吧，但不知道身處這裏已經有多久，至少也有幾天了。我身處的這個房間很小，像個監獄，有幾個放蠟燭的位置，牆上刻著一個巨大的五角星。

這裏有很多男男女女走來走去，他們把食物和便壺拿給我然後又拿走。有時候他們會忘記拿食物給我，我以為這是最糟糕的事。

我每天只有麵包和清水充飢，有一次我抱怨說自己還是很餓，他們告訴我可以吃蟑螂來補充蛋白質，我以為這是最糟糕的事。

I think they drug me quite often. A few times I've passed out suddenly, and when I wake up, my body hurts. Sometimes I have bruises and cuts without knowing where they came from. I thought this was the worst thing.

The drugging, passing out, waking up with injuries has been getting worse. This last time, I woke up with two pentagram–shaped burns, one on each forearm. I thought this was the worst thing.

They treat me better now. I still try not to think about why. I get more food, candles, a few extra blankets to sleep on. Then, my belly started to swell. I thought this was the worst thing.

One night, I am ripped out of my sleep by a ripping pain coming from below. I scream at the concrete walls. I keep screaming and screaming until they come. I don't get any drugs this time. I feel split in half, before God and everyone. The pain is so bad I forget how much I hate Mr. Colton and his cronies as they tend to me. I beg for them to kill me. It takes hours before the baby comes out. I thought this was the worst thing.

I rest, and they take the baby away. I have no interest in the baby. I want to go home.

我猜他們應該常常向我下藥吧。有好幾次我突然昏倒過去，到我醒來時都會渾身疼痛。有時身上又會有一些不知名的瘀青和傷口，我以為這是最糟糕的事。

下藥、昏倒、醒來發現受傷的情況愈趨頻繁。最近一次是我醒來時，發現身上多了兩個五角星型的燙傷，分別燙在我兩隻前臂上，我以為這是最糟糕的事。

他們現在待我好一點了，但我還是盡量不去想為甚麼。他們現在會給我多點食物，會多放點蠟燭，也多給我幾張被子，讓我睡得好一點。在這之後，我肚子開始脹起來，我以為這是最糟糕的事。

有一晚，我在睡夢中痛醒過來，一股撕裂的痛楚從下而來。我對著四面牆尖叫，一直聲嘶力竭地尖叫著，叫到他們過來為止。這次他們沒有給我任何藥物，我好像在眾目睽睽之下被撕成兩邊似的。我痛不欲生，也痛得使我忘卻了我有多痛恨 Colton 先生和他的同黨。我甚至哀求他們殺掉我。折騰了多個小時後，寶寶終於出生了，我以為這是最糟糕的事。

我放鬆了下來，他們把寶寶帶走了。我不在乎寶寶，我只想回家。

But one day, I hear footsteps approaching my prison. They tell me everything will be OK as long as I do one more thing.

The scream that erupts from my throat is louder than any noise I made in childbirth. They bring me a platter with a tiny, frail human figure on it, the flesh charred and blackened.

They tell me to eat. This is the worst thing.

但有一天，我聽見牢房外有腳步聲正在靠近。他們告訴我一切都會好起來的，只要我再多做一件事就行了。

從我喉嚨爆發的尖叫聲比分娩時更慘烈……他們拿了一隻大盤子過來，盤子裏盛著一個細小脆弱、呈燒焦發黑狀的人形物體。

他們叫我把它吃掉——這才是最糟糕的事。

A Day Off in Hell

Hell is a room with two doors.

The first shuts behind you as you step inside. It locks into the frame, never to open again. The second door stands at the opposite wall, a solid implacable barrier, its purpose utterly inscrutable.

As soon as both doors are closed, your torment commences. The room houses a single unique punishment, dealt out at the deft sadistic hands of your custodian. You will scream, you will cry, and as you watch your wounds heal just enough to keep the pain fresh, there will be nothing you'll want more than escape.

Once you have endured 24 hours of punishment, you are permitted a day off.

The second door will swing open, revealing a bare, soft lit room. Any time you wish you can pick yourself up and shuffle, unimpeded, through the doorway into the grey stone room. The space is featureless except, as always, for two doors.

As the door shuts behind you, your wounds will heal, your pain will subside and for 24 hours, nothing will happen. There are no special comforts, but in the quiet absence of

地獄休息日

地獄是間有兩扇門的房。

你進去之後，第一扇門就會關上，並會牢牢鎖上，不會再打開。第二扇門立在第一扇門對面的牆上，像是一座堅固不移的障礙物，作用不明。

當兩扇門都關上時，折磨環節便會開始。這個房間有一個很獨特的懲罰方式，像是把你從百般呵護的溫室裏趕出來，沒有人再會給你庇護。這裏會使你尖叫、哭泣；那些傷口會保持在剛受傷的狀態，令痛楚持續不散，而你滿腦子都只會想著要逃離這裏。

經歷過持續二十四小時的虐待後，你可以獲得一整天的休息時間。

此時，第二扇門會徐徐打開，裏面是個散發著柔光的空房間。當你終於能撐起身體勉強走動時，你就可以隨著那暢通無阻的門口，走到灰色石房間裏去。這個房間的間隔不變，仍然有兩扇門。

當門關上後，你的傷口會逐漸康復，接下來的二十四小時內，你所有的痛苦都會消退，亦不會發生任何事。雖然沒有甚麼安慰或優待，但不需再受持續的折磨，對你而言已經有

ceaseless torment you drink every second like ambrosia.

Here's the thing however. When your time is up, when the second door opens and you are pulled inside, you will be in a new room, with a new tormentor and, importantly, your new punishment will be noticeably worse.

Some take a while to notice the pattern. Some notice immediately but just can't take the pain. They dash through the door as soon as it opens, eager for a day of peace. Those people have it the worst. They descend quickly beyond the realms of imaginable suffering, and their yearning for release will only make those 24 hours more inadequate. All of them will start to think of their earlier punishments almost fondly, lamenting that they ever set foot in the grey room but unable to stop.

But the real trick is played on those who learn restraint. Those who realise the bone rending torment they're undergoing is better than anything beyond the grey room. Their heart breaks a thousand times, every moment they decide not to step into that next room. Their soul shatters the moment they decide they're going to stay in that room.

Hell is a room with two doors.

如瓊漿玉液般難得，也會使你意猶未盡。

不過，當時間一到，第二扇門打開的時候，你就會被拉進去一間新房間，體驗一番新的折磨，而且更重要的是，這個新的懲罰會明顯比之前的更痛苦。

有些人需要過一段日子才會發現這個規律，有些人很快就發現了，但還是抵不住痛苦煎熬，他們會為求一日安寧，在門開啟時馬上衝過去。但這群人是最慘的，他們會急速從安寧中崩塌，承受比想像中更痛苦的折磨。他們那顆渴望解脫的心，只會使那安寧的二十四小時更顯短暫。頃刻之間，這群人全部都會覺得之前的懲罰原來已經算是溫柔得多，同時痛恨自己為何要把腿踏進灰色房間。

真正耐人尋味的地方，是在於那些學會克制的人。他們明白到，雖然現在正承受刻骨銘心的痛，但仍然比踏進灰色房間後的懲罰好得多。每當他們決定不要踏進灰色房間之時，都會心碎一次，而這樣的情境重複了千遍萬遍。當他們決定要留在原本房間那一刻，他們的靈魂就已經破碎了。

地獄是間有兩扇門的房。

The first shuts behind you as you step inside. It locks into the frame, never to open again. The second door stands at the opposite wall, open and waiting. Reminding you with every agonising second, that this is a Hell you chose.

你進去之後，第一扇門就會關上，然後牢牢地鎖起來，不會再打開。第二扇門就立在對面的牆上，敞開著，等待著。這扇門每分每秒也在提醒著你，這個地獄是你自己選的。

You Need to Eat

"You have to eat, honey. You need your strength."

But 13–year–old Adalyn didn't want to eat, never again. Nothing stayed down anymore. She had been unable to keep food down for years. Just the smell of the homemade chicken soup caused a fresh supply of bile to rise.

She pushed the bowl away and closed her eyes. "I don't want this," she said. "Where's the nurse?"
"She left 30 minutes ago while you were still asleep."

Adalyn tried to move to a comfortable position, something almost impossible to do with the IV and all the tubes hooked up throughout her body. She groaned and tried to lie down.

"Don't do that. You need to eat."
"I'm not hungry."

"Your lack of hunger is what got you here. Everyone is worried about you. It's wrong to starve yourself."

Adalyn sighed. She knew better. Even if she wanted to eat she couldn't keep anything down. She could never keep anything down, not since she was a little girl.

厭食症

「你要吃東西啊親愛的，吃東西才有力氣啊。」

但十三歲的 Adalyn 不想進食，也不肯再吃東西。她總是會把食物都吐出來，這樣的情況已經持續了很多年。單單是聞到自製雞湯的氣味，就足以使她把黃膽水通通都吐出來。

她把碗子推走，然後閉起雙眼。「我不想吃這個，」她說：「護士呢？她在哪裏？」
「她三十分鐘前走了，那時你還未醒來。」

Adalyn 試著轉到一個舒服點的姿勢，但那幾乎是不可能的，因為她身上插著很多靜脈輸液管，那些管子在她身上纏成一團，使她無法轉身。她煩厭地嘆了口氣，嘗試躺回床上。

「不要這樣，你要吃東西才行。」
「我不餓。」

「正是因為你不覺得肚子餓，才會住在這裏啊。每個人都很擔心你啊，讓自己捱餓是不對的。」

Adalyn 又嘆了口氣，她也很清楚自己的狀況，就算她想進食，最後也是會吐出來。她從小開始就會把吃進去的食物全都吐掉。

"Everyone is so worried about you."

I bet they are, she thought.

The nurse walked in, to Adalyn's relief. "Hello, sweetheart! How's our patient?"
"Fine," she said without enthusiasm.

"She's doing much better," her mother said as she applied a fresh coat of dark lipstick, "but I can't get her to eat."

The nurse looked up from Adalyn's chart and then placed it back in its spot to the side of the hospital bed. "Don't worry, Mrs. Anderson. We can put her on a controlled diet here. You don't have to keep bringing stuff in."
"But she's had severe food allergies," her mother broke in, "and I can't be sure what you all give her won't make her worse."

Adalyn observed the exchange. They had been through this before. She had never been allowed to have hospital food. Why would she get lucky this time? The nurse gave her a glance, and Adalyn looked at her with desperate and pleading eyes.

「大家都很擔心你啊。」

他們當然擔心我吧，她心想。

護士走了進來，Adalyn 如釋重負。「甜心你好！我們的病人怎麼樣了呢？」
「很好。」她平淡地回答。

「她好很多了。」Adalyn 媽媽邊塗著深色唇膏，邊說著：「但無論我怎麼勸導她，她還是不肯吃東西。」

那護士查看了一下 Adalyn 的病情紀錄，然後把它放回病床旁邊。「Anderson 太太，你不用擔心，我們可以為 Adalyn 度身訂造餐單，幫她控制飲食，你不用每次都拿食物過來啊。」
「但她有嚴重的食物過敏啊，」她媽媽打斷了護士的話，「我怎麼知道你們給她的食物會不會令她病情惡化啊？」

Adalyn 注意到她們的爭論，她們之前也試過這樣吵起來。Adalyn 的媽媽從來不讓自己吃醫院的食物。這次又怎會是例外呢？護士瞧了她一眼，Adalyn 就以一副絕望和哀求的眼神回望她。

"Really," the nurse went on, "we can take care of her if you want to go home and rest for a few hours."

The veins in Mrs. Anderson's face bulged out. "Are you insane! I am her mother! There is no way I will leave her side!"

The nurse shrugged and left the room.

Adalyn blinked back her tears. It was always the same thing. Her mother pushed the bowl of soup toward her again, only this time she wore a look of frightening authority. "Adalyn Nichole Anderson, you need to eat and eat now. Don't make me tell you again!"

She reached out with her bony arm, now noticing as if for the first time just how frail she had become. Adalyn picked up the spoon full of soup and raised it to her mouth. The smell of household cleaner mixed in brought on fresh nausea. By now her mother was busy on phone.

"Yes... Thank you for your prayers... I know, but having a sick child is my cross to bear..."

「不會的，」護士小姐接著說：「如果你想回家休息幾個小時的話，我們會照顧她的。」

Anderson 太太頓時青筋暴現，「你瘋了嗎！我是她的媽媽！無論如何我也不會離開她半步！」

那護士聳了聳肩就離開了病房。

Adalyn 眨眨眼，收回眼淚，心裏暗忖著「每次都是這樣」。她媽媽把那碗湯再推前給她，這次媽媽的臉上展露出可怕的威嚴。「Adalyn Nichole Anderson，你要吃東西才行，馬上給我吃。我只說一次，不要讓我再說第二遍！」

Adalyn 伸出瘦骨嶙峋的手，就像初次發現般，察覺到自己原來變得多麼的虛弱。她拿起了湯匙，把它放近嘴邊。混在湯裏的家用清潔劑氣味使她作嘔。此時她媽媽正忙著聊電話。

「是的⋯⋯感激你們的祈禱⋯⋯我知道，但有個生病的孩子確實是個沉重的負擔⋯⋯」

The Beep Test

"The Multi–Stage Fitness Test will start in one minute." An audible groan rises from the class as we take our places on the starting line. Everyone I know hates the Beep Test – unless a 20–meter, back–and–forth shuttle run is your idea of fun. As I go to take my spot, Mr. Collins pulls me aside.

"Now, I don't want to see any slacking from you this session, Matthews."

Feigning confusion, I furrow my brows quizzically. "I don't know what you mean, sir" I lie. "I'm just a bad runner."

"The purpose of this test is to determine your physical potential, and my job to make sure that you reach it" he growls. "I know you have it in you to be the best – but you're never going to achieve anything by being lazy."

I roll my eyes. He's right, of course. I am lazy. Every year, without fail, I intentionally get myself knocked out of the Beep Test second – after the resident fat kid – so I can relax on the sidelines. What can I say? Glorified time–trials don't motivate me in the slightest.

"Start Level 1.1" chimes the boombox.

The class takes off in a light jog. True to form, Billy

地獄式體能訓練

「多段式體能測試將於一分鐘後開始。」班上的同學邊抱怨著，邊走到起跑線上，一字排開。我認識的每個人都很討厭來回跑，除非你覺得不斷在那二十米距離內跑來跑去很好玩吧。我站到自己的位置後，Collins 老師把我拉到一旁。

「聽好了 Matthews，我不想再看見你在這個項目偷懶。」我皺起眉頭，裝作一副疑惑不解的樣子。「老師，我不懂你的意思啊？」我撒謊道：「我真的跑得很慢啊！」

「這個測試是為了判定你的身體潛能，而我的職責是要確保你能通過測試。」他咆哮著說：「我知道你可以做到最好，但如果你耍懶的話，你就永遠都不會有所成就。」

我翻了白眼。他說得沒錯，我的確很懶惰。雖然每年的體能測試我都及格，不過我每次都故意讓自己在來回跑中成為第二個被淘汰的人，排名剛好在那個常常首先被淘汰的胖子後面，然後我就可以舒舒服服的在球場邊休息，不用再跑了。那我還有甚麼好投訴呢？只是這種計時賽對我來說一點都不吸引，我也毫無動力去練習。

「第 1.1 階段開始。」揚聲器鳴響著。

我們全班一起慢跑著。一如既往，那個胖乎乎的男同學 Billy

Stephenson, the chubby one, is knocked out first at Level 4. However, instead of me, this time Lana Cooper is the second to go. Then Daniel Broderick, and then Shelly White. By Level 9, half the class has been eliminated from the test. Yet, for once, I'm still running. And I'm hardly even breaking a sweat. Eventually, it's down to just me and Alex Munroe, the class fitness nut. It doesn't take long for her legs to give out, sprawling in a heap as I dart over the line.

"Start Level 13.1."

Grinning madly, I feel a wave of pride wash over me. 13.1. Never in my wildest dreams would I have thought that I would get to Level 13 in the Beep Test. In my moment of fulfillment, I almost forget how I got here.

Bang! A gunshot fires into Alex's back, silencing her exhausted gasps.

Spurred on, I continue bounding across the gym, leaping over the bullet–ridden corpses of my less–nimble classmates. I glance back to our gym teacher, a wide grin on his face and a smoking pistol trained on me.

Mr. Collins was right. I really did have it in me to be the best. All I needed was the right motivation.

Stephenson，在第 4 階段首先被淘汰了。但是接下來第二個被淘汰的不是我，而是 Lana Cooper，然後到 Daniel Broderick，再到 Shelly White。到了第 9 階段，已經有半班同學不能通過測試了。然而，這是我第一次還在跑。我幾乎不費吹灰之力便撐到現在。最後，只剩下我和另一位運動白痴 Alex Munroe 還未被淘汰。不過當我衝過終點線之後，她的雙腿很快就會筋疲力盡，然後攤在地上，動彈不得。

「第 13.1 階段開始。」

我瘋狂的獰笑著，突然感覺到有股自豪感湧現。13.1 了！我做夢也沒有想過自己可以在來回跑中撐到第 13 階段。在我享受著滿足感的時候，幾乎忘記了我為何能撐到第 13 階段。

*呼！*子槍穿越了 Alex 的背部，使原本氣喘吁吁的她，再沒有發出聲音。

我很鼓舞，繼續橫越著體育館，跨過一個又一個因為笨拙而被射死的同學們的屍體。我回望著我們的體育老師，臉上掛著燦爛笑容的他，用一根冒著煙的手槍瞄著我。

Collins 老師說得很對，我真的可以做到最好。我只是需要一個適當的動力。

Poor Boys

"Thank you so much for letting me in", Michael said as he wrung rainwater from his shirt. The thunder boomed outside again.

"Nonsense, sweetheart," the old lady said, smiling warmly.

"I've taken in plenty of poor unfortunate boys over the years. Oh, I mean, you are leaving as soon as you can, of course, but it's rare to see such a sweet little gentleman, I'd keep you if I could. Now let me fix you some tea to warm up with while I see if I can find you something dry to wear." She stopped to stroke Michael's cheek.

The woman herded him inside to a nice little living room and sat him down at a table. A kettle was already boiling on the stove. She poured something from a coloured tin container into the kettle, picked up two tea cups and their saucers and twirled around to set the first one before Michael, the other opposite of him. There was some scar on her hand. A bite mark?

"I'll be back in a jiffy!" she gleamed as she dashed off elsewhere in the house.

As Michael was sitting awkwardly and sipping his tea he heard something else approaching in an uneven shuffle. It was a boy, hobbling forward with a cane before half–sitting, half–

避雨

「你人真好，肯讓我進來，非常感謝你！」Michael 邊從他的襯衫上扭下雨水邊說著。轟雷又怒哮了一聲。

「別客氣啦，親愛的。」那老太太面帶微笑，熱情地回應。

「這麼多年來我接收過不少可憐又不幸的男孩了啦，噢，我是說，你當然可以隨時離開，但像你這般可愛的小紳士真的很罕見呢，真想把你留在這裏！我去弄點熱茶給你取暖吧，順便看看有沒有一些乾淨的衣服給你穿。」老太太摸了摸 Michael 的臉頰。

老太太帶了他進去一個漂亮的小客廳，叫他坐在餐桌那邊。爐子上的水壺已經燒開了，老太太將一個有色錫容器裏的東西倒進水壺，拿了兩隻茶杯和茶碟，然後走到 Michael 面前放下一杯茶，再把另一杯茶放在對面。她手上有些疤痕……是咬痕？

「我很快回來！」她眼睛閃閃發光地說，然後又蹓走了。

Michael 尷尬地坐在餐桌旁喝著茶，聽見了有些跌跌撞撞的聲音正在靠近。原來是個拿著拐杖、步履蹣跚的男孩，半坐半倒的跌坐在 Michael 對面的椅子上，雙目無神地盯著二人中間的餐桌。

collapsing to the chair the opposite of him, staring blankly at the table between them.

"Uh, hi", Michael said, but the pale boy did not raise his eyes or show a sign he had heard. At first Michael guessed he was somewhere around his own age, but there was something withered and sickly about him.

"Oh, you've already met my sweet little Wilhelm!" the woman said as she returned with her arms full of clothes. "I'm sure you'll make great friends." She set the pile of clothes on an unoccupied chair, stroked Wilhelm's hair and kissed his cheek. The boy didn't look up, smile, or even dodge her. She poured him tea as well and headed off again for something she apparently remembered.

"So, uhh... How old are you, Will?" Michael tried asking, setting his empty cup down.
"I'm thirty–four," Wilhelm answered with a pained, raspy voice. "You didn't drink that, did you?" He looked at the cup, and then up at Michael. His eyes were completely dead.

Michael opened his mouth, but found himself unable to speak. He could not feel his legs. Somewhere behind himself, he heard a door click shut.

「呃⋯⋯你好。」Michael 跟他打招呼，但那蒼白的男孩沒有回望他，也沒有任何反應，好像聽不到他講話似的。Michael 猜想著那男孩應該跟自己差不多年紀吧，但那男孩好像很憔悴，一臉病容似的。

「噢，這個是我親愛的 Wilhelm 呢！」老太太拿著一大堆衣服回來，「我敢說你們一定會成為好朋友！」她把那堆衣服放到一張沒人坐的椅子上，摸摸 Wilhelm 的頭髮，然後親了親他臉頰。那男孩沒有抬頭，沒有笑容，也沒有退縮。老太太也給 Wilhelm 倒了茶，突然想起遺忘了些甚麼，於是又走開了。

「嗯⋯⋯呃⋯⋯Will，你今年幾歲了？」Michael 放下他的空杯子，試著問 Wilhelm。
「我三十四歲。」Wilhelm 以一把痛苦、刺耳的聲線回答。
「你沒有喝那個吧？」Wilhelm 望著那隻杯子，然後再望向 Michael，但他的雙眼已再無半點生氣。

Michael 張開了嘴巴，但發現自己不能說話，雙腿也沒有知覺了。在他後方的某處，傳來了關門聲。

But I'm Not Bitter

We had a huge party for my little brother last summer, on his sixth birthday—moon bounce, water balloon fights, a cookout, and of course, a gigantic cake.

My party will be much, much smaller—just a cake, really—and even for that, Mom didn't have any flour to make the batter.

But I'm not bitter. I jog briskly down the road to the Parkers'— "Just run down quickly, and see if they have any flour, then hurry right back", Mom says. "And wear your raincoat, and gloves, Laura..."

I glance up at the sullen grey clouds that seem to have covered the sky forever, and doubt that a raincoat and gloves will offer much protection.

I knock on the Parkers' front door when I arrive, feeling silly. Mrs. Parker will likely be just where she was when I came here last, sprawled on the kitchen floor, covered in weeping, seeping sores, with a few rats gnawing at her face....

And that's where she is still, though since it has been over a week since I was here, she is now mostly bone, with some clinging gristly bits, and she doesn't care at all as I grab the whole canister of flour, and the bag of sugar she had in the pantry. The bombs, with their poisonous vapors and plague–

但我沒有不滿

去年夏天，為了慶祝弟弟六歲生日，我們給他辦了個大派對。那天我們玩了吹氣城堡、水球大戰、吃了露天燒烤，當然還少不了一個巨型蛋糕！

我的派對則相對地非常非常簡陋——只有一個蛋糕，沒其他了，媽媽甚至沒有麵粉來做麵糊。

但我沒有不滿。我迅速地跑過去 Parker 夫婦的家。「趕緊跑過去，看看他們有沒有麵粉，然後快點回來。」媽媽吩咐道：「Laura！記得要穿雨衣，還要戴上手套啊……」

我望上天空，那些灰濛濛的雲層似乎要把天空永遠蓋起來，然後心裏暗忖著雨衣和手套是不是真的能保護我。

我跑到 Parker 夫婦門前敲了敲門，有種犯傻的感覺。Parker 太太應該還在上次我過來時看到她的位置，那時她四肢攤開，躺在廚房的地上，滲滴著膿液的瘡滿佈全身，還有幾隻老鼠啃噬著她的臉……

雖然上次過來已經是一個多星期前的事了，但她現在還是躺在那邊。Parker 太太已經差不多只剩一副白骨，骨上還依附著一些軟骨組織。即使我從食品儲藏室裏拿走了整筒麵粉和一大袋砂糖，她也完全不在乎。當時那些炸彈連同有

clouds, caught most of us unaware, but Mrs. Parker believed in always having a well-stocked pantry.

I leave quickly, not wanting to see if Mr. Parker is still alive. Last time, he was crying and begging me to take him with me, but I couldn't get his wheelchair down the stairs, and lost control of it—he tumbled to the bottom, but I heard him groaning as I ran out the door, so I know he was alive then.

The rats probably have gotten him by now. I don't even check, just run out the door again, and home with the flour and sugar.

Mom finishes mixing up my cake, and lights a fire to bake it, while I put Desitin on the worst of the sores on my brother's face and arms, and then treat my own. They are worse today, and probably being outside didn't help, even with a raincoat. In a month or so, we'll probably be dead as the Parkers, who had no cellar to go into when the bombs came.

My cake smells wonderful as it bakes. My brother drew me a sweet picture of us fishing together, and Mom even found candles for my cake. This will most likely be my last birthday party ever.

But I'm not bitter.

毒氣體和大量雲層向我們襲來，大多數人也毫無防範，但 Parker 太太一向未雨綢繆，有個儲備充足的食品儲藏室。

我急步離開，不想知道 Parker 先生是否還活著。上一次他哭著哀求我帶他一起走，但我不懂如何把坐在輪椅的他推下樓梯，途中還失控……他摔了下去。但我跑到門口的時候聽見他呻吟的聲音，所以我知道他還未死。

那些老鼠現在應該在咬他了吧。我沒有去查看，只是跑到屋外，帶著麵粉和砂糖回家。

媽媽拌好了給我做蛋糕的麵糊，然後點起了火準備烤焗。同時，我替弟弟臉上和手臂上那些最嚴重的瘡塗上紓緩乳膏，然後再替自己塗。今天好像變嚴重了，可能出外沒甚麼幫助，就算穿了雨衣也無補於事。再過一個月左右，我們應該會像 Parker 夫婦般死去，我們兩家人都沒有地下室，遇到炸彈襲擊時一樣無處可逃。

焗爐傳出蛋糕香噴噴的味道，弟弟畫了一幅畫送給我，是我們一起釣魚的溫馨畫面。意外地，媽媽也找到了蠟燭，插在蛋糕上面。這次大概會是我最後一個生日。

但我沒有不滿。

Privatization

"Hello! You've reached the hotline for St. Michael's Police and Security, protecting and serving since 2018! If you need to request police services because of an ongoing incident, please press ①. If you want to make a monthly payment, please press ②. If you would–"
①

"You've requested police services because of an ongoing incident. If this is a violent crime, press ①. If this is a property–"
①

"You've reported an ongoing violent crime. If this is correct, press ① now, or say, 'Yes.'"
①

"For the best and most timely service, please type in your Customer Service Number now."
⑨③⓪②⑧④⓪⓪②

"I'm sorry, we've detected an unpaid claim on your account of $259.99. In order to reinstate your account, please contact the billing department. Thank you for calling St. Michael's Police and Security."

警力私有化

「您好，歡迎致電 St. Michael 警察及保安部熱線，我們自 2018 年起一直保護及服務市民！如閣下因現正發生的事項需要警方支援，請按①字；如欲繳付月費，請按②字；如需⋯⋯」

①

「您已選擇『因正在發生的事件需要警方支援』。如該事件為暴力罪案，請按①字；如該事件為財物⋯⋯」

①

「您已報告一宗『正在發生的暴力罪案』。如資料正確，請按①字，或者回答『是』。」

①

「為確保最佳和最及時的服務，現請輸入閣下的客戶服務號碼。」

⑨③⓪②⑧④⓪⓪②

「很抱歉，根據紀錄，閣下的帳戶內尚有一項未繳款項，金額為 259.99 元。如閣下想恢復的帳戶，請致電計費部門，感謝致電 St. Michael 警察及保安部熱線。」

Emergency Eclipse Instructions

Please forward this to **EVERYONE** in the path of the total eclipse today, August 21, 2017 immediately.

NASA and the United States Government have released the following statement.

<u>A NOTICE TO ALL INDIVIDUALS
IN THE PATH OF THE TOTAL ECLIPSE</u>

· Do not look directly at the sun during the eclipse, regardless of the use of protective eyewear.

· Please seek immediate shelter during the eclipse. If you are unable to be indoors during or immediately following the eclipse, please do not try to contact emergency personnel, friends, or relatives.

· If you come into contact with anyone outside during or immediately following the eclipse, do not make any form of contact.

· Immediately following the eclipse, do not make any noise louder than a whisper until you are retrieved by emergency personnel.

日食緊急指引

請立即將此指引轉發給今天（2017 年 8 月 21 日）**所有**會外出觀賞日全食的市民。

美國太空總署及美國政府發佈了以下聲明：

<u>致所有外出觀賞日全食市民之通告</u>

・無論有否佩戴防護眼鏡，日食期間切勿直視太陽。

・於日食期間請立即尋求庇護。如閣下在日食期間或日食剛完結時無法走到室內，請勿嘗試聯絡任何人，包括緊急救援人員、朋友或親戚。

・如閣下在日食期間或日食剛完結時在外面遇到其他人，不要作出任何形式的接觸。

・在日食剛完結時，請保持肅靜，直至有緊急救援人員尋回閣下為止。

· When emergency personnel attempts to make contact, do not respond right away. Wait until you are sure that the person making contact is real.

· In the event that no contact is made by the emergency crew in the 48 hours following the eclipse, stay inside as long as your provisions allow before venturing outside.

· If you notice any strange rashes on your skin or any thoughts you believe may not be your own, quarantine yourself at once.

We apologize for the short notice, and hope that this message doesn't get out too late.

May God forgive us.

・如有緊急救援人員嘗試跟閣下接觸，不要即時作出回應。請耐心等待，直至閣下確定該人員是真實的，方可作出回應。

・如在日食完結後四十八小時內沒有緊急救援人員跟閣下接觸，請在許可情況下盡量留在室內，不要冒險外出。

・如閣下發現自己身上出現奇怪的疹子，或出現閣下認為「不屬於自己」的想法，請立即隔離自己。

我們為此向公眾道歉，還望此訊息不會散播得太遲。

願上帝原諒我們。

A Letter From
the Previous Homeowner

I just closed on a house this morning! After years of saving and planning, my wife and I were finally able to get the money together for the down payment and closing costs that come with buying a house.

While my wife and I were moving boxes in that first day, I happened to open the mailbox. I'm not sure why I did it – for anyone who's ever owned a house, you may understand the strange compulsion to open all the doors and explore all the nooks and crannies, so I opened the mailbox.

Inside my new mailbox was a letter, addressed to me specifically, with no postage or return address. I've transcribed it below.

I cannot begin to tell you how sorry I am for what you're about to read. If you're a family man, which I believe you are, I trust that you'll understand the gravity of my situation after reading this letter. I did what I needed to do in order to protect my family – even if that meant condemning another.

If what I've been told is true, it's just you and your wife moving in – no children of which to speak – which is the only solace I have in selling you this house.

There are certain things you must know about this house, many of

前屋主的信

我今早剛剛買到房子了啦！這麼多年來，我們一直辛辛苦苦存著錢，也計劃了很久，我和太太終於可以用這筆錢應付首期和過戶費用，確確實實的把房子買下來了！

第一天入伙時，我和太太忙著把一個個箱子搬進屋裏。突然我心血來潮，想打開郵箱看看。我不知道為何自己會這樣做，但如果你曾經當過屋主的話，你可能會理解到那股奇怪的衝動，它會使你想打開全屋子的門，使你想去探索每一個角落、每一道縫隙。於是我就打開了郵箱。

我的新郵箱裏頭有一封信，註明是給我的，但信封上面既沒有郵戳，也沒有回郵地址。我把信的內容寫出來給你們看吧。

對於你接下來將會讀到的內容，我只能表示無限的抱歉。如果你是個有家室的男人，不過我想你正是吧，我相信你讀完這封信就會明白我的現況有多危急。我現在所做的一切都只是為了我的家人，儘管這樣做會傷害到另一個家庭也好，我也別無他法。

我絕無半點虛言。如果真的只有你和你太太會搬進來，也即是沒有孩子的話，這回事就是唯一令我良心好過點的安慰。

有關這間房子，有幾件事你是需要知道的，但有很多我現在

*which I cannot write even now, but if you do **EXACTLY** what I've laid out below, there shouldn't be anything to worry about.*

1. Do not allow children on your property. I cannot stress this enough. No trick–or–treaters, no Christmas carolers, no babysitting.

2. Always leave one light on in the basement.

3. If you misplace anything, do not look for it.

4. Always set an extra place at the dinner table.

5. If you have pets, especially dogs or cats, make sure to lock them up in a secure cage at night and when you are away.

6. Make sure you are in bed between the hours of 3 and 4AM with the bedroom door closed.

Again, I am terribly sorry and I hope that you follow these directions to the letter. Please don't be angry with me – I was only trying to get my children back.

I want to believe this is a cruel joke, but every time I look at this letter, my stomach turns. The part that scares me the most is the first bullet point. **Do not allow children on your property.** He may have done his research on my wife

*也無法寫給你，不過只要你**緊守**以下提及到的規矩，那就沒甚麼好擔心了。*

1. 孩子不得進入物業範圍內，這點是極度重要的。不准有萬聖節嘩鬼，不准唱聖誕歌，不准有保姆。

2. 地牢必須留有一盞亮燈。

3. 如果你忘了東西放到哪裏了，不要去找。

4. 飯桌必須多留一個空位。

5. 如你有飼養寵物，尤其是狗隻及貓隻，在晚上及外出時請務必把牠們關在籠子裏。

6. 在凌晨三時至四時這段時間內，你必須已在床上，並且謹記關上房門。

我再一次表示我很抱歉，亦希望你能跟從以上提及的指引。請不要生氣，我只是想救回我的孩子而已。

我多想這只是個殘酷的笑話，但每次再讀這封信時，我也不禁嘔吐大作。最讓我驚怕的是第一點：**孩子不得進入物業範**

and me, but I don't think his research was extensive enough to know that my wife is currently nine-months pregnant – she's due within the week, and the doctor said she could go into labor any day now.

I wish I could just get out of the house, but literally everything I had went into buying it, so for now my wife and I are stuck here...

圍內。那個前屋主應該有調查過我和太太，但我不認為他的調查會深入到知道她現在懷有九個月身孕，而且預產期是今個星期，醫生提醒過我們寶寶隨時都可能會出生。

我真希望我可以逃離這間房子，但我現在名副其實地，花光了自己的性命財產來買這房子，所以現在我和老婆就困了在這裏⋯⋯

Virulent Delusion
極 端 妄 想

Baxter Didn't Recognize Me

When I walked through the door today, the dog didn't recognize me. There was no rush to greet me or enthusiastic tail wags. Instead he growled softly. I walked toward him, hand outstretched and palm down.

"Hey, boy. What's wrong?" I asked him.

He bristled as I approached, curling his upper lip almost imperceptibly.

"Okay, okay. I get it," I said as I walked to the kitchen. I poured myself a drink as I considered the situation. That was not like Baxter at all. Maybe he was sick, or maybe he hurt himself. Whatever the cause, he had started barking at me. I couldn't figure out why his demeanor would have changed so radically from the dog I knew.

I thought about calling the vet, going so far as to pull the magnet with the phone number off of the refrigerator, before the clock caught my eye. It was close to six, and Michelle would be home soon. She'd know what to do, and we could decide together about Baxter.

I stood in the kitchen sipping on my rye and soda, listening to Baxter's increasingly hoarse barks. I could barely hear the click of a key in the lock. Michelle was home, thank god. I sat

Baxter 不認得我了

今天回家時，狗狗不認得我了，牠沒有跑過來歡迎我，也沒有熱情地搖尾巴，反而是輕聲地咆哮著。我走向牠，嘗試伸手撫摸牠。

「喂，乖寶寶，你怎麼了？」我問道。

我向牠走近，但牠卻豎起了毛，還漸漸地咧起嘴來。

「好吧好吧，我懂了。」我邊說邊走到廚房。我倒了杯飲料，然後細想著那是怎麼回事。那樣根本不像 Baxter，可能牠生病了，又或者受傷了吧。雖然不知道甚麼原因，可是牠開始向我吠叫。我不理解為何牠會突然變成這樣，完全不像那隻我熟悉的 Baxter 了。

我想帶牠去看獸醫，正打算走到雪櫃把那個貼在櫃門上的電話號碼拿下來。走向雪櫃的途中我望到了時鐘，差不多六點了，Michelle 很快就會回來。她會知道該怎麼辦，然後我們就可以一起商量有關 Baxter 的事。

我站在廚房邊喝著威士忌混梳打，邊聽著 Baxter 愈漸沙啞的吠叫聲。我隱約聽見鑰匙插進門鎖的聲音，Michelle 回來了，太好了！我把杯子放在料理枱上，聽著她高跟鞋敲著瓷磚地板的咯咯聲。

my drink on the counter and listened to the click, click, click of her heels on the tile floor.

"Baxter? What in God's name are you barking at?" She yelled from the living room. Baxter turned from me and ran to greet her. I couldn't help but feel a little jealous.

Michelle walked toward the kitchen, with Baxter leading the way and barking. I could hear her approaching slowly, with caution. I almost yelled out to her, to tell her that it was all right. That it was just me. Instead, I held my tongue.

When she turned the corner to the kitchen, she screamed. That was so unlike her.

"Who the fuck are you? What are you doing in my house?"

I shushed her, shaking my head as I walked toward her. This is not at all the reaction I expected. It was almost as if she didn't want us to be a family.

"It's okay," I said in my most soothing tone of voice. "I was a little bit concerned about Baxter, and I wanted to know if we should take him to the vet?"

Michelle began to cry. "How...how do you know my dog's

「Baxter，你在吠甚麼鬼啊？」Michelle 在客廳叫喊道。Baxter 轉身背向我，然後跑向 Michelle 歡迎她。我不得不承認自己有點吃醋。

Baxter 邊吠邊帶著 Michelle 走過來廚房，我聽到她戰戰兢兢地逐漸走近。我差點就想大聲跟她說沒事，只是我在這邊而已，不過我還是止住了。

當她轉彎到達廚房時，她失聲尖叫著。這真不像她⋯⋯

「你他媽的究竟是誰？你在我家幹甚麼？」

我示意她安靜下來，我搖搖頭走向她身旁。這根本不是我預期的反應，她好像不想我們成為一家人似的。

「沒事的，」我盡可能用最平緩的語氣安撫她：「我有點擔心 Baxter，所以在想是不是應該帶牠去看獸醫。」

Michelle 哭了起來：「你⋯⋯你怎麼會知道我狗狗的名字？」說罷，淚珠便沿著她漂亮的臉龐徐徐滾下。

name?" she asked, tears streaming down her beautiful face.

It broke my heart, it really did. Did she think she was alone in the world, that no one would be there to help her when she needed it? Like, for example, when there was something clearly wrong with our dog.

As Baxter continued to bark, I approached her and gathered her up in my arms. "Shh," I whispered into her hair as she struggled against me. "It's all right now. We're a family, and everything is going to be all right."

這使我心碎了⋯⋯難道她真的以為自己是孤獨一人，在她需要幫忙時，沒有人會伸出援手嗎？就像現在，我們的狗狗很明顯是有甚麼不妥啊！

Baxter還是吠個不停，我靠近她，張開雙臂把她擁進懷裏並道：「噓⋯⋯」雖然她想掙脫我，但我仍然輕聲細語道：「現在沒事了，我們是一家人嘛，一切都會好起來的。」

I'm Not Suicidal, I'm Just Testing Her

I can't quite recall when she first showed up. I remember when I was a child, running, screaming into my parent's bed. I just remember blubbering to them about the girl under the bed. The girl that looked just like me. My Mum just ruffled my hair, told me I was being silly and to go to bed. I tried to sleep. But I could hear her.

Whenever I rolled over, she would too. It didn't stop. When I woke up the next morning, so did she. I went to school. So did she. The thing about her, was that although she was identical to me, nobody else could see her. She wasn't a ghost…as such. Nobody could see her, but she was still human.

She was a copy–cat though. Every. Single. Thing. I did, she would do too. I became prone to her, her soft voice that was identical to mine, the way that although she might be in a different place to me, she would be doing the exact same thing.

When I was younger, all of my other friends had friends that nobody else could see. Yet as we all grew older, their friends went away, mine did not. I called her Copy–Cat, Cat for short.

隱形的自己

我已經不記得她從哪時開始出現，只記得小時候每次看到她，我都會尖叫著跑到爸媽的房間。也記得我會跟他們哭訴，說床下有個女孩，而且那個女孩跟我長得一模一樣。媽媽會摸摸我的頭告訴我，不要再亂想了，然後叫我快點回去睡覺。我努力入睡，但我仍能聽見她活動的聲音。

我轉身，她也轉身，不斷模仿著我；隔天早上我起床，她也起床；我上學，她也上學。但最讓我懊惱的是，雖然她長得跟我完全無異，但沒有任何人能看見她。她不是鬼魂，應該不算吧。雖然沒有人看見她，但她還是個人類。

她根本就是個 A 貨，我每・做・一・件・事，她都會照樣模仿。我沒辦法無視她，她柔弱的聲線跟我一模一樣，有時候雖然她跟我身處不同地方，但她仍然模仿著我的一舉一動。

我年紀還小的時候，我其他的朋友全部都有其他人看不見的隱形朋友。但隨著年齡增長，他們的隱形朋友逐漸消失了，但我的「朋友」還在。我叫她做 A 貨，簡稱小 A。

When I was 12, I wanted to see how far she would go to copy me. I stole a razor from my Dad's bedroom and brought it to my wrist. I know I shouldn't have done it, but I needed to know just how far Cat would go. I slit my wrist, just scratching the surface to start off with but then going deeper. Still, Cat copied.

I don't know what happened next, just waking up in a pool of blood, my Dad calling an ambulance. The next few months were a blur, with Mum and Dad talking to therapists and specialists, thinking I was 'self harming' and 'depressed'. That's stupid though, I just wanted to see how far Cat would go.

I began to test Cat even more, I would cut deeper. Different places and more frequently. Cat would always do it. I got scissors, cut all my hair off. Cat did it too.

And now I'm here. My feet teetering on the edge of the chair, rope wrapped loosely around my neck. It won't be loose soon. I stare at Cat, she is on an identical chair, with an identical rope with identical clothes and an identical expression. I just want to see how far Cat will go.

十二歲時，我想試探一下她能模仿我到甚麼程度。我從爸爸的睡房裏偷了把剃刀，然後放到自己的手腕上。我知道我不該這樣做，但我真的很想知道，小A能模仿我到甚麼程度。於是我割開了手腕，最初只是割著表皮，但之後愈割愈深。小A還是照樣模仿著。

之後的事我就不清楚了，只記得自己在一片血海中醒過來，然後聽見爸爸打電話叫救護車。接下來的幾個月我都矇矇矓矓，只知道爸媽接見了很多個治療師和專科醫生，說我有「自毀傾向」和「抑鬱」症狀。胡說八道！我只是想試探小A能模仿我到甚麼程度而已。

我試探小A的次數愈來愈多，傷口也割得愈來愈深。我在不同的地方試驗著，也愈試愈頻密。小A也依舊模仿著。我拿起剪刀，剪掉自己的頭髮。小A也剪掉自己的頭髮。

現在我搖搖晃晃的站在椅子邊緣，頸上有條鬆鬆的繩圈，不過很快就不會是鬆鬆的了。我瞪著小A，她站在跟我一樣的椅子上，圈著跟我一樣的繩子，穿著跟我一樣的衣服，臉上掛著跟我一樣的表情。我只是想試探小A能模仿我到甚麼程度而已。

Besides, Mum and Dad are taking me away tomorrow…they said something about me being mentally deranged, suicidal, something like that. They're so stupid. I'm not suicidal.

I just want to see how far Cat will go.

I kick the chair from under my feet.

The rope tightens instantly.

Cat steps off her chair.

而且爸媽明天就要把我帶走了，他們説我精神失常，又説我有自殺傾向，一堆諸如此類的説話。他們真的很笨，我沒有自殺傾向。

我只是想試探小 A 的能耐。

我把腳下的椅子踢走。

繩子馬上扯緊了。

小 A 從椅子上走了下來。

I Didn't Turn up for My Mother's Funeral

Bottles of whiskey, drained of their content. Blood and bandages strewn across the floor, the knife's blade crusted over with dried brownish–red patches. My arms sting from the cuts I had inflicted from self–harm.

And yet I couldn't get up and pull myself to the funeral of the woman I cared for most in the world.

Was I a bad son for not turning up to see her off at the gates of her final journey? I don't think so. I was there when she died, after all, and funerals are for the living, not the dead.

Was I a bad son for not replacing the batteries in the house alarm? I hope not. Nobody could have known the batteries were faulty; I would have changed them in a heartbeat if I had known.

Was I a bad son for pulling a gun on the burglar, and threatening to take his life? I don't know. My mother didn't raise me to be a murderer, but that speaks more about me as a man than as a son.

They say parents have a sixth sense that allows them to detect when their children are in danger. She had rushed into my room, at that time.

我缺席了母親的喪禮

一瓶瓶空了的威士忌、血跡和繃帶佈滿地上。啡紅的斑點凝固在刀刃上。我手臂上那些因自殘而造成的傷口正隱隱作痛。

但我無法收拾心情，也沒有出席她的喪禮，即使她是這個世界上我最關心的女人。

我沒有陪著她走過人生最後一程，我算是個壞兒子嗎？我不覺得我很壞，因為她死去的時候我有陪在她身旁。畢竟喪禮是為活人辦的，而不是為了死去的人而辦。

我沒有替家中的防盜系統換上新的電池，我算是個壞兒子嗎？應該不算吧。誰會想到那些電池竟然是次貨呢？如果我早知道的話，我一定會立即把它們換掉。

我拿起槍指著那個小偷，並威嚇會把他殺了，我算是個壞兒子嗎？我不知道，媽媽把我養大成人，不是想我當個殺人犯。這不只是從作為兒子的層面來說，而是從作為男子漢的層面來說。

有人說父母有股第六感，當子女身陷險境時，他們就會感應到。那時候，她衝進了我房間。

The wind howls outside, reminiscent of the bullets that had been fired that night. One from the housebreaker, and a whole lot from me, I presume. We fired at exactly the same time. I couldn't recall anything past the blood rushing through my head.

I remember my mom throwing herself in between us to shield me from the bullet.

Papers litter the floor around me; from the police, from the laboratories.

Was I a bad son? I don't want to find out, but then again, the letters pull at me like gravity to a meteor.

One bullet had ended my mother's life. I don't want to know whose it was.

外面寒風凜冽，讓我回想起那晚橫飛的子彈。有一顆子彈屬於小偷的，我猜其餘的都是屬於我的。我們同一時間扣下了扳機，那刻血液沖昏了頭腦，我不知道發生了甚麼事。

我只記得媽媽飛身撲向我和小偷中間，為我擋子彈。

地上有很多報告圍滿了我，有警察給我的，也有實驗室給我的。

我算是個壞兒子嗎？我不想知道。但那些信件像隕石墜落般狠狠打擊了我。

一顆子彈結束了我母親的生命。而我不想知道那子彈是屬於誰的。

My Daughter Never Ran Away

My daughter, Katy, never ran away. I don't know why they keep telling me that.

It was her teacher that notified the police. She said that Katy had left her a note. A note saying that she was scared, that she needed to get away.

My daughter, Katy never ran away, they need to stop saying that.

I prop my legs up against the coffee table, watching the presenter warble on. They are still talking about Katy, about *my daughter*. I stare over at her now, she is curled in the corner. She's crying, but it's just a joke between her and me. That's what parents do. They make jokes with their kids like that. "Come here, Katy," I say, beckoning her with my finger. She lets out a loud sob "take me home, who are you? Please. Just take me home." I laugh, shaking my head. Katy and her jokes.

My daughter, Katy, never ran away. She came home. She is home now.

I just wished she would start calling me mother.

我女兒沒有離家出走

我女兒 Katy 沒有離家出走，我不懂他們為甚麼老是説她離家出走了。

那時候報警的是她的老師，她説 Katy 留了一張字條給她，字條上寫著她很害怕，她很想離開。

我女兒 Katy 沒有離家出走，他們不要再這樣説了。

我把雙腿晾在茶几上，聽著電視裏的人在吱吱喳喳。他們還在説著關於*我女兒* Katy 的事。我望向瑟縮在角落的她。她在哭，但這只是我和女兒的小玩笑而已，其他父母也是這樣的啊，他們也會跟自己的子女開玩笑。「過來吧，Katy。」我招手示意她過來。她大聲抽泣著：「讓我回家……你到底是誰？拜託你，讓我回家……」我聽見 Katy 開的玩笑，不禁笑了起來，然後搖搖頭。

我女兒 Katy 沒有離家出走，她回家了，她現在在家了。

我倒是希望她會肯開口叫我一聲「媽媽」。

Dementia & Chopsticks

When I walk into my mother's kitchen, I sigh. The first thing I see is a brown bag and a pile of chopsticks on the counter. My sister must have gotten Chinese for them tonight.

My mom's voice, breezy and lilting, floats in from the living room. "Your father and I ordered food, honey. Are you hungry?" I don't respond. Her words an unwitting blade puncturing my good mood.

My father loved to cook with chopsticks. I remember watching him as a little girl, effortlessly flipping the chunks of meat and vegetables in a wok with the little wooden sticks. My mother (ever the pragmatic one) made a point to grab some extra chopsticks whenever she happened to encounter them, knowing my father's preference.

But my father's been dead for almost eight years now, and my mother's dementia is getting worse. Among the many unexpected, painful things that come up when a loved one has dementia, one of them was my mother's insistence that Dad is still alive and still wanted extra chopsticks.

痴呆症與筷子

我走進廚房時不禁嘆了口氣。第一眼看到的，就是料理枱上有個啡色的袋子，還有一堆筷子。肯定是妹妹買了中式晚餐回來。

媽媽活潑輕快的聲音在客廳裏迴響著：「親愛的，我和爸爸買了食物回來，你餓了嗎？」我沒有回答。她的話像刀刃般劃破了我的好心情。

我爸爸很喜歡用筷子做菜，我記得小時候看著他用鑊和那兩枝木棍子輕鬆地翻轉肉排和蔬菜。媽媽（以前沒有患病時）如果看到有筷子可以拿的話，都會多拿幾雙筷子給爸爸，好讓他可以用來做菜。

但我爸爸八年前已經死去了，而媽媽的痴呆症也愈來愈嚴重。心愛的人患上了痴呆症，會發生很多意料不到、使你心痛如絞的事。其中一件使我很痛苦的事，是媽媽堅持爸爸仍然在生，還想要拿額外的筷子給他。

Nine months ago, my mother got into a screaming match with the delivery guy because he (not understanding her condition) refused to give her another pair. I'll never forget holding my mom as she collapsed on the floor, sobbing and wailing, "I need them for your father. Where is your father?"

Now they just give us extra chopsticks, wordlessly.

I am snapped out of my reverie when my phone rings, loud and brash. Fumbling, I dump my bag on the table and fish out the device. My forehead wrinkles. It's my sister, which makes no sense, because today was her day to take care of Mom.

"Did you get my voicemail?" she said breathlessly. When I say no, in confusion, she lets out a spirited, "*Fuck!* There was an emergency at work and I had to come in at lunch today. I was able to get Mrs. Penrose to come sit with her, but she couldn't stay for the whole evening. I called Sam, but he was at home because Jenny had a cold. Has Mom been alone all night?"

Her words fade off until they sound like they are underwater. Slowly, I look around the kitchen. It looks normal, but I was so distracted by the damn chopsticks that I didn't notice the huge, muddy boot prints coming in from the patio door.

九個月前，媽媽曾經跟一個外賣員吵起來，因為他（不了解她的病情）拒絕給她多一雙筷子。我永遠都忘不了那時她跪倒在地上，悲痛地哭泣著：「我要拿筷子給你爸爸……你爸爸在哪裏？」

現在那些外賣員都會默默地多給我們幾雙筷子。

急速而響亮的電話鈴聲把我從沉思中驚醒過來。我慌忙地把袋子放到桌子上，摸索著找電話。我皺起了眉頭，是妹妹打電話來。不可能的啊？今天是她負責照顧媽媽的啊……

「你有聽到我的語音留言嗎？」她氣喘吁吁地說。我疑惑地答了沒有，她立刻破口大罵：「*他媽的！*今天公司有突發事件，所以我中午就要趕去上班。我有拜託 Penrose 太太過來陪她，但她不能整晚都留下來。我也有打給 Sam，但他要留在家照顧病了的 Jenny。媽媽整晚都自己一個人在家嗎？」

她的話愈來愈模糊，像是在水底裏說話般。我緩緩地望向廚房，沒有發現甚麼不妥。但那些該死的筷子使我分了心，令我忽略了那些從院子那邊的門走進來、巨大而黏滿爛泥的靴子印。

If You See Me,
You Should Probably Kill Me

I'm an abomination.

But we can't help our natures, can we?

That's not rhetorical. Some parts of our own being exist outside of our control, like the fact that my heart beats 85 times a minute when I sleep. Others are entirely within our own volition, such as the words that I choose to type.

But the confounding reality is that most of our actions are a mixture of both. How many regrettable things have you said after drinking? Did you blame it on the alcohol while knowing it really was all your fault?

I can't speak for everyone, because everyone chooses a different nature. But during the low point of my monthly cycle, I'll admit that I choose to act differently.

It's in my nature.

I'm not proud of who I become, but I let it happen anyway. In the moment, the decisions I make seem to be logically sound. When that cycle ends, though, I look back in horror at what I did. And in my regret, I promise that I will never make the same mistakes again.

請殺掉我

我是個神憎鬼厭的生物。

但江山易改，本性難移，對吧？

我並沒有誇大其辭，因為我們身體有些部分就是無法自控的，就像我睡覺時，心跳高達每分鐘八十五次，我也控制不了。其餘部分我們則很自由，就像我現在選擇打甚麼字一樣，可以自行作主。

但事實上，上述兩種情況均會在我們大部分行為中出現。你記得喝酒後說過多少讓自己後悔的話嗎？明知是自己的錯，你還會說只是酒後亂性，與自己無關嗎？

我不能代表所有人，因為每個人都有不同的本性。但到了每個月週期性的低潮時，我承認我會選擇表現得比較不一樣。

那是我與生俱來的本性。

我變成了另一個模樣，雖然我對此並沒有很自豪，但我也隨遇而安。我在那些時候做的所有決定都似乎很合理可靠。但當那個週期一完結，我就會發現那些決定有多離譜，使我後悔莫及。我發誓我不會再重複犯錯了。

Then the cycle begins anew. I can *feel* myself becoming different. Neurotransmitters flood my brain, making me decide to *decide* to behave in ways that I normally never would. Those are the times when I wonder if there really is a soul peeking just behind the curtain, hoping its voice can be heard over the distracting hum of brain chemistry. In my lower, more desolate moments, I cynically believe that the "soul" *is* the brain chemistry. That what we imagine to be something *greater* is nothing more that neurological synapses arranging themselves in a protective stance that delays but never denies the inevitability of mortality.

Does that make terrible decisions easier or harder to live with?

I'm nearly at the end of my most recent cycle. Right now, I feel no guilt for how much I have ignored the suffering of the people around me. I know that I could have used my position to save a life. It would take so little. I could reach into my bank account right now, empty it out, and a thousand starving people would eat tonight.

But I won't do it, and I won't feel bad about it.

That's just my nature.

當新的週期再來時，我能感覺到自己有所變化：腦內的神經遞質不斷流動，使我決定要顛倒自己的本性，做一些平時不會做的事。我曾經在想，會不會真的有個靈魂偷偷的躲在窗簾後，盼望著有人會聽到它的聲音，腦海會因而受到影響。有時候當我感到很低落淒涼時，我又會變得很憤世嫉俗，認為腦袋*正正就*是「靈魂」的本體。我們以為*更偉大神奇*的東西，其實只不過是那些神經突觸在保護機制之下自行排列，而推遲了，但沒有違反「生物必死」的準則。

這樣的話，那些離譜的決定是會變得無關痛癢，還是會變得更難接受呢？

現在我的週期已經差不多要結束了。我無視了那些因為我而受害的人，而且我一點也不內疚。我知道我本可利用職權來拯救生命，根本不費吹灰之力。我也可以把銀行戶口裏的存款統統提出來，足以餵飽成百上千的飢民。

但我不會這樣做，而我也不會因此感到難過。

因為這是我的本性。

I'll regret it soon, though. My cycle will end, and I will return to my natural state of simply not caring about a dollar or material possessions. In those moments, I wish I could be free of my physical belongings forever, and know that I was the richer for it.

For now, though, I am going to ride out the last few hours of being the most selfish creature that ever lived. There's not much full moon left, and I'm determined to wind it down without hurting anyone. It's the best that someone of my kind can hope for.

I just can't wait for this full moon to end, so that I can change from a human back into a wolf.

但我知道我很快就會後悔了。我的週期快將結束，然後就會回到原本的狀態，毋需再理會任何錢銀瓜葛。在那些時刻，我希望可以不再受物質財富約束，可以明白及謹記心中富有這個道理。

不過，我作為世界上最自私生物的身份只剩幾個小時而已。月圓已經快不見了，我決心要平靜下來，不傷害到任何人。這是我和我的同類最想達成的共同願望。

我很期待月圓快點結束，那我就可以從人類變回狼了。

Home Alone

I'm not quite sure why, but even in my adult years staying home alone fills me with a sense of anxiety.

Ever since I was a kid and my parents would stay out late, or even in college when my roommates hadn't yet returned from Christmas break, something didn't seem right about being home alone.

It was almost as if the idea of being the only person occupying so much space was impossible.

Rooms and beds unoccupied, accompanied by what feels like a cautious and uncertain sense of privacy.

Something always seems wrong when I stay home alone, but that's not really what scares me anymore.

What scares me is my roommate has been gone this whole week. And I feel just fine.

獨自在家

不知怎的，就算現在長大成人了，一旦家裏只剩自己一人的話，我就會很焦慮不安。

小時候當爸媽很晚才回家，我就會有這種感覺，或是大學時室友回家過聖誕還未回來，我也會很不安，總之我獨自在家就會渾身不對勁。

那個感覺就像自己一個人不可能佔用到這麼大的空間似的。

房間和床鋪都是空的，卻有一種被人看光的不安感。

當我一個人在家，我就總是覺得有甚麼不妥，可是這也再算不上讓我害怕的事了。

真正嚇倒我的，是室友已經整個星期都不在了，但我卻覺得好好的。

He Deserved to Die

My husband and I are sitting in the living room, finishing a bottle of wine, when he stands and shuts the curtains abruptly. I give him the look, and he nods back at me. Peeking past the curtains, there he is: a dirty, disheveled man with dried blood adorning his skull, neck, and shoulders. His name was Chris Kleck, and seven months ago, I killed him.

I should note that I killed him in self–defense, while he was attempting to rob me and beat my husband to a pulp. But still, I killed him. I took a human life.

We were on vacation in New York City, walking home from dinner, when it happened. He hit me once and I fell – he must have assumed I was down for the count, because he immediately went to work punching my husband. The sounds of Chris's knuckles pounding into my husband's skull were so horrible I thought that alone would render me insane.

But it didn't, and I ended up tackling Chris, holding his arms so he couldn't break his fall. I remember the sound his head made on the pavement – it sounded so ordinary, kind of like the distant thud of free weights I'd heard at the gym. I was speechless when the police told me later that he'd died.

他是該死的

我和老公坐在客廳，喝完了一瓶酒。他猛然站起來關上窗簾。我望著他，他點了點頭。我透過窗簾望出去，看到了「他」。他是個骯髒、衣衫襤褸的男人，他的頭、頸和肩膀都沾滿了血跡。他的名字是 Chris Kleck，七個月前，我殺了他。

我要說明一下，我是出於自衛才殺他的。他那時對我們行劫，又把我老公打得血肉模糊。但終歸，我的確是殺了他，我了結了一條生命。

那時候我們在紐約度假，吃完晚餐正在走路回家，然後 Chris 就走過來搶劫我們。他打了我一下，我跌倒了在地上，他肯定以為我會被打一下就倒地不起，因為他立刻轉身走去打我老公。Chris 的拳頭打在我老公頭上的聲音實在太可怕了，我以為這種聲音已經足以把我逼瘋。

但我很冷靜，跑了過去擒抱著 Chris，試圖把他摔倒。我緊緊地按著他兩條手臂，不讓他掙脫。我還記得他的頭撞向路面的聲音——聽起來很平常，就像是在健身房裏會聽見，那些啞鈴被拋在地上的那種悶響。後來警方跟我說他死了，嚇得我說不出話來。

We decided not to tell the family all of the details. Our story was that my husband was the victim of a robbery, not much had been stolen, and the mugger had gotten away.

But a few days after we'd arrived home, Chris started showing up in our yard. It was confusing because none of our security cameras could record him, and it didn't appear that any of our neighbors saw him either. We live in the kind of uptight community where yard signs and exterior paint choices can cause irreparable rifts, so when no one called the police on our strange visitor, we assumed that we were just going crazy.

Seven months of this, and he never moves. He just stands there and stares at the house, at us.

My husband and I finish our wine as the headlights of my sister's car temporarily flood the room with light. We hear her cheerfully lock the car, walk up the porch, let herself in.

Both of us start upright when she says innocently, "So who's the weirdo in the front yard?"

我和老公商議好不跟家人透露任何細節。我們說好了事情是這樣的：我老公是搶劫案的受害者，那個搶劫犯沒有搶到甚麼，然後就逃走了。

可是我們回家後幾天，就看到了 Chris 在我們的院子裏出現。但奇怪的是，我們的保安攝影機全都沒有拍到他的影像，其他鄰居也似乎沒有看見他。我們住在一個鄰里關係緊張的社區，無論是院子標誌，還是外牆塗料的選擇也足以使左鄰右舍出現分歧，而且他們之間永遠不會和好。所以當我們家門前出現了一個奇怪的陌生人，但也沒有人報警，我和老公以為只是我們自己發瘋了。

七個月過去了，他絲毫沒有移動過。他只是站在那裏，瞪著房子，瞪著我們。

我和老公剛剛喝光了酒，妹妹的車頭燈就照亮了整個房間。我們聽見她輕快地鎖上車門，走到門廊，逕自走了進來。

妹妹呆頭呆腦地問了一句話，震懾了我們：「話說前院的那個怪人是誰啊？」

A Game of Hide and Seek

Behind my house was a large field of dry grass and bushes. My mother always hated it when my little brother and I played there because she was worried about us getting hurt, but she never really stopped us.

The grass was tall – up to my thigh in some places, and was perfect for playing hide–and–seek. One of us would count to a hundred, and the other would run as far as he could and dive into the grass, laying perfectly still and listening to the rustle of the other's footsteps as he searched.

We would play this for hours some days when it wasn't too hot, and even at night when we could manage to get out.

In the center of the field stood a large, dead tree, which was always where the person counting stood. That day it was my little brother's turn to count. He rested his face against the trunk of the tree and counted backward from a hundred as I sprinted through the dry grass.

I could hear his voice in the twenties now and was preparing to hit the ground when my foot caught something and I was sent hurtling down toward the earth. With a painful thud, I hit the dirt. I went to cry out for my brother to stop the game, but as the dust from my fall cleared, I found that I could no longer speak.

捉迷藏

我家後面有一大片乾草叢和灌木叢，媽媽很討厭我和弟弟跑到那裏玩耍，因為她很擔心我們會受傷，不過她從未禁止過我們。

那些乾草很高，有些更到我的大腿位置，非常適合玩捉迷藏。我們其中一人會由一數到一百，另外一個就會跑走，有多遠跑多遠，然後躺在草叢裏，一動不動地聽著「鬼」來捉自己的腳步聲。

如果天氣不是太熱的話，我和弟弟都會玩上幾個小時，甚至在晚上，我們也會出去玩。

那片草叢中間有一棵很大的枯樹，那是負責捉人的鬼數數時會站的位置。那天是弟弟當鬼，他趴在樹幹上，背對著我，然後從一百開始倒數，我就立即在草堆中拔腿狂奔。

我聽見他已經數到二十幾了，有些東西絆倒了我，使我整個人快仆倒在地上。隨著一聲悶響，我就躺在地上。我本想大叫讓弟弟暫停遊戲，但在那些揚起的塵土散去後，我發現自己吭不出聲音。

Inches from my face, staring back at me with dried eyes, was the thin, pale face of my little brother. The skin on his face was dry and taut and his teeth shone through thin lips like a grimace. Flies buzzed in and out of his ears, nose, and eyes and I wanted to scream. But what stopped me was the distant voice behind me, counting backwards from a hundred.

"Four!"
"Three!"
"Two!"
"One!"
"Ready or not, here I come!"

Author: Ben Asper (DoverHazelt) **176**

一張離我只有數吋的臉正用「他」乾枯的眼睛狠瞪著我⋯⋯
那是弟弟一副很瘦弱、蒼白的臉容。他的皮膚既乾燥又緊
繃，薄薄的嘴唇下露出閃亮的皓齒，跟他扭曲的臉龐形成對
比。蒼蠅從他耳朵、鼻子和眼睛飛來飛去，我很想尖叫。但
令我呆著的，是在我背後那正在倒數的聲音⋯⋯

「四！」
「三！」
「二！」
「一！」
「躲好了沒有？我來捉你啦！」

Tap Tap Tap

I lay in bed, covers pulled up to my chin and eyes glued straight up to the ceiling.

TAP TAP TAP

I wouldn't look over. I wouldn't and I couldn't. If I did, I just knew that it would be over. My eyes burned to dart over to the right; to look out of the window and see what there was to see.

TAP TAP TAP

Sweat beaded on my brow, and eventually spilled over into my eye. I blinked rapidly but kept my eyes trained on the ceiling. I stared so hard at it that my vision began to turn grey around the edges. I needed to sleep, but there was no way I could do that while it was out there, waiting for me to look at it.

I yearned to know. My young mind told me that knowing would be better than this – this terrifying and gnawing misery of the knowledge that it was there, looking at me, while I was powerless to do anything about it. I stared at the ceiling.

TAP TAP TAP

嗒嗒嗒

我躺在床上，把被子蓋到下巴位置，雙眼凝視著天花板。

嗒、嗒、嗒。

我不會望過去的，我不會，也不能。我知道如果我望過去，一切就會完結了。我眼睛超想滾去右邊，望向窗外，看看那邊有甚麼東西。

嗒、嗒、嗒。

汗珠凝在我眉頭，然後流進眼睛。我快速地眨眼，但雙眼依然盯著天花板。但我望得太入神了，視野邊緣漸漸變成灰色。我很想睡覺，但只要「它」一刻還在外面，我就一刻也不能睡著，因為「它」在等我望向它。

我很想知道那是甚麼。我幼小的心靈在想著：「與其像現在無能為力，甚麼也做不到，不如看看這個可怕又折騰的東西是甚麼吧。」但我還是死命地盯著天花板。

嗒、嗒、嗒。

It dragged across the glass of my bedroom window, causing a squeaking noise which set my bones on edge and made me want to leap out of my own skin. I pulled my feet up, crossing them like they had us do in school. I'd suddenly wondered if there might also be something under my bed, and the thought of it reaching up to grab my feet and pull me under was too much to bear.

The time dragged on and on. I had no idea of the actual hour or minute, since my clock was on the nightstand to my right and to look at it would mean looking at the **thing**. The **it**, whatever **it** was. I had the sense of time passing, but it could have been seconds, hours, or days for all I knew.

Shapes danced in the darkness around me. I suddenly became aware that I hadn't heard the tapping in some time, and I wondered if it had gotten in. Had I left the window open, even just a crack? Had it slipped in, and was it now in the room with me? I slammed my eyes shut and pulled the covers over my head. I could feel it looking at me, drawing ever closer to my bed, waiting for me to peek from beneath the covers so it could spring at me and tear me to pieces. I held my breath.

它沿著我睡房窗的玻璃拖行著，發出刺耳的吱吱聲，毛骨悚然得讓我的骨頭好像要從皮膚裏撐出來似的。我把腿縮起來，像學校老師教我們般盤起腿來。因為我突然驚覺不對勁，想著會不會也有甚麼東西躲我床下，我很怕它會伸手上來抓住我的腳，這個想法把自己嚇壞了。

時間一分一秒地過去，我不知道實際過了多久，因為放在床頭櫃的時鐘在我右邊，我望過去就等於我會望到那個**東西**。那個**它**，不管**它**是甚麼也好。雖然我感覺到時間流逝，但不知道是過了幾秒、幾個小時，還是幾天。

影子在黑暗中圍繞我舞動著。我突然意識到已經有一段時間沒有聽到那些嗒嗒聲，我才驚覺它是不是進來了⋯⋯我是不是打開了窗，哪怕只是開了一條縫？如果它溜了進來，現在不就跟我一起在房間裏面？我立刻緊閉起雙眼，把被子拉起來蓋過頭。我感覺到它在看著我，慢慢靠近我的床，等待著我從被子裏偷看它，逮到我之後就會跳到我身上把我撕成碎片。想到這裏，我屏住了呼吸。

Suddenly there was a loud, screeching *BOOM* against the glass of my window. Unable to bear it any longer, I threw the covers from my head and sat up, staring directly out the window. Better to die looking it in the face and knowing what it was than to continue this agony.

The branches of the tree outside my window rustled in the wind as the storm built, and as they recoiled back, they struck the glass.

TAP TAP TAP

突然間窗戶玻璃傳來了一聲刺耳的巨響，*呼！*我再也按捺不住了，我把被子扔到大腿位置，坐直了起來，直直的盯著窗外。我寧願在死也想看到它的真面目，我不想再繼續備受煎熬。

窗外的樹隨著風力漸強沙沙作響，當那些樹枝在風中搖曳時，就會撞到玻璃。

嗒、嗒、嗒。

BOOK OF NO SLEEP　無眠書2

編 譯 解 讀

以下僅為個人理解，並不一定或完全代表作者原意。

死亡真相

天台的瘋子 • 12
主角很享受被人注視的感覺，但他不是要跳樓自殺，而是要把另一個女人推下去。

寂靜之聲 • 14
主角的朋友在聽覺未恢復之前，一直都在「聽見」別人的尖叫聲。

安息 • 15
主角就是殺女子的兇手，而棺材是空的，因為主角把女友的屍體藏了在衣櫃內。

迷途小男孩 • 17
呼應「黑眼兒童」的都市傳說，幸好主角沒有讓那些怪物進入房子，否則就會被它們帶走了。

救命被單 • 19
黑暗中的怪物是真的，只是主角的弟弟跑得不夠快，被抓走了。

病毒 • 20
主角被受病毒感染的工具割傷了，所以盡責的他也在受感染人數上加了一。

婊子血腥瑪莉 • 22
主角不慎把 David 嚇至失足墮樓了，只好當作是血腥瑪莉的詛咒應驗了。

酒後亂性 • 25
主角喝醉後就會吃人，那個紋身

男就此喪命於主角的肚子裏了。

先是尖叫聲，然後是笑聲，再來是電鋸聲 • 27
與主角關係密切的某人被綁架了，但因為主角本來準備好的贖金被偷走了，於是綁匪就撕票了。

夢想成真 • 29
燈神一諾千金，把主角的「夢」都實現了，可惜主角的夢全是惡夢，得不償失。

掘屍真相 • 31
主角掘屍時發現屍體全部都翻身向下，似乎想向地底逃走，暗示了有甚麼將會在天上襲來，危害人類。

癌症治療 • 33
母親不想患癌的兒子受苦，親手殺掉了他，卻在三天後聽見了有關癌症治療的廣播，受不住打擊自殺了。

約會真人秀 • 35
主角參加的真人秀節目其實是個殺人活動，參加者被「淘汰」後就會被殺，幸好主角發現不妥後成功逃離，不然就會跟其他人一起葬在莊園了。

混蛋小孩 • 37
畫作裏丟石頭的鬼男孩其實是隻好鬼，保護著其他孩子，但樹被砍掉之後他消失不見了，所以現在黃衣鬼女孩可以肆意作惡了。

遇見死神 • 40

死神選中主角不是要他死去,而是要他成為新一任的死神。

擬娩症候群 • 43

Michael 不知道妻子 Fecilia 原來是外星人,在它們的族群裏只有雄性才會生小孩,所以 Michael 是真的懷孕了。

全都稀釋掉 • 45

精神病院內的病人都不是真正的患者,而是被醫生注射了奇怪的藥劑。到主角去探望她時,也不幸被醫生「治療」了。

沙漠公路 • 48

有人把 Eddie 的臉皮割下來了,還披在自己的臉上裝成 Eddie 本人。主角懵然不知,一直與他駕車同行,後來聽見車尾廂的怪聲才發現真正的 Eddie 已經遇害。

壞女孩 Julia • 50

那兩個高大男人是警察,他們來到 Julia 家想拘捕殺了郵差的爸爸,但不幸被肚子餓的 Julia 吃掉了。

請無視我的自殺 • 52

主角是位患有創傷後遺症的退伍軍人,生無可戀的他想自殺,但同時他會把試圖拯救自己的人當成敵人殺掉,所以衷心希望別人無視他的自殺。

情愛妄想症 • 54

Jack 沒有聽從 Quiro 女士的吩咐而把魔藥喝光,令他變成了「萬人迷」,被那些女人瘋狂追捧,甚至想讓 Jack 和自己同歸於盡。

鄰里同樂節 • 57

主角自己和鄰居們全都是罪犯,住在這裏沒有人會冒險舉報對方,使各人十分安心。

雙生兒 • 59

這對雙生兒的心靈和身體也相通,家人埋葬了 Janet,但其實她本來還未死,曾經在棺材裏掙扎,而這一切都反映在 Jill 的身體上。

報案室奇趣錄 • 61

來電者跟蹤了接線員 Alice 很久,甚至住在她家的牆壁裏。來電者打電話到 Alice 工作的地方,是為了讓她知道自己的存在,宣稱自己會繼續不斷騷擾她,決要在她心裏烙下永不磨滅的陰影。

睡前故事 • 65

主角女兒會學習故事的「教訓」,而主角不小心說得過了火的故事,就成了女兒最新的學習對象,挖了不同動物的眼睛弄成冠冕。

好朋友的承諾 • 67

主角答應了好朋友 Ronald 要讓他成名,想到如果 Ronald 死了一定能引起公眾注意,於是狠心殺掉了他。

他又來了 • 70

故事上半段是主角母親的視角，患上老人痴呆症的她不斷重演著童年的回憶，「窗外的老太太」其實就是鏡子裏的自己。最後醫生更揭發了主角母親是受到主角爺爺 Joshua 的虐待，導致精神創傷。

辣手報復

天生殺人狂 • 75

Billy 是主角剛出生的兒子，但主角嫌他太煩，瞞著男朋友殺了他。

強制性安樂死 • 76

首相下令全國實施「強制性安樂死」害死了主角的女兒，所以當首相要求作為神經外科醫生的主角替他做手術時，主角「不慎」令手術失敗，讓首相自食其果。

賢妻 • 78

Elnora 其實有聽見丈夫求救，只是她見死不救，被死去的丈夫發現後要她償命。

小鎮大事 • 80

主角在萬聖節當天把毒藥混進糖果派給小朋友，最後被居民圍捕，選擇服毒自殺。

我不是象人 • 83

主角因為患病、長相與別不同而遭受歧視，於是發揮「象人」食肉的本性，把觀眾們吃掉了。

音訊全無 • 85

David 痛恨母親年輕時沒有善待自己，於是現在報復她，把有老人痴呆症的母親鎖在房裏，也堅決不回信。

不像其他女生 • 87

Laura 一早知道 Josh 是個變態，與他交往只是為了拯救妹妹，並把他處決。

母親的愛 • 90

主角從小到大都有媽媽「保護」，把欺負自己的人都禁錮起來施虐，主角知道反抗也會被媽媽懲罰，於是繼續默許媽媽的行為。

我已竭盡所能 • 93

主角和 Clay 雖然母子關係疏離，但得悉 Clay 把女孩抓去禁室培慾後，主角看不過眼，要親自處決兒子。

廿四孝丈夫 • 96

John 不只把主角的妻子殺死了，之前還有十四名受害人。主角作為好好先生，現在就替那些受害人報復，把 John 關在地下室裏虐待至死。

不算最慘的死法 • 99

Kiera 所幹過的事都不符合爸爸媽媽說死得最慘的例子，接下來她也不會讓妹妹經歷「最慘的死法」。

七宗罪之憤怒 • 101

主角母親一直包庇父親的暴力行為，直到母親被父親打至昏迷後，主角就諷刺父親的橫蠻，以「發洩怒氣」為由，把父親殺掉。

腦外傷後
人格劇變的現象很普遍 • 103

經歷嚴重事故後人格突變，是因為本來的「人」已經死去，身體卻被其他靈魂侵佔了。

無情背叛

相依為命 • 107

Frank 是隻狗狗，但牠不再是人類最好的朋友了，因為牠捱不了餓，把 Stanley 吃掉了。

少女拍賣會 • 110

面具男雖然受聘找回 Leslie，但其實他也是個人販子，表面上是救走 Leslie，實際上是將 Leslie 收歸己有。

私奔 • 113

可憐的 Katie 以為 Mark 是真命天子，離家出走跟他私奔，可惜最後被 Mark 虐殺了。

愛妻心切 • 115

主角打算自殺來騙取保險金讓妻子可以過更好的生活，但走到窗台時又想退縮，豈料妻子「幫」他一把，讓他墮樓。

紋身的故事 • 116

主角的媽媽不願將主角交給社福機構，更打算割掉主角的手腕，同歸於盡。

孩子安靜才乖 • 119

因為主角的母親嫌主角太吵了，於是剪掉了主角的舌頭，再把他的雙唇縫起來，這樣就可以樂得清靜了。

男朋友的怪癖 • 121

男朋友買大量蠟燭回來是為了可以召喚死去的前女友，然後與前女友和主角三人一起繼續生活。

我是個乖女兒 • 124

主角很聽爸爸的話，所以當爸爸變成了活死人之後，很乖巧地把爸爸殺掉了。

稻草人 • 126

主角殺掉了爸爸，然後把他插上木柱，變成了稻草人，繼續看守著自己的麥田。

姊姊又佔著浴室了 • 128

主角的姊姊 Amy 早在三年前已溺死了，但至今仍然冤魂不散，常常佔著浴室。

困境抉擇

抉擇 • 132
主角正面對一個比一個更難接受的心理關口，到底該選擇放棄生存，還是繼續自殘，等待奇蹟來臨呢？

最糟糕的事 • 135
主角被鄰居拐走後不斷被虐待，但那些經歷不算最糟糕，最糟糕的是施虐者要主角吃掉自己的骨肉。

地獄休息日 • 138
下地獄的人是罪有應得的，無論如何也要受折磨，但你會寧願不間斷地受苦，還是休息過後接受更慘烈的折磨呢？

厭食症 • 141
Adalyn 的母親為了博取他人同情，一直強迫 Adalyn 吃有毒的食物。

地獄式體能訓練 • 144
教練的地獄式訓練非常奏效，正所謂「適者生存」，跑得不夠快就要死！

避雨 • 146
老太太專門「收留」不幸的男孩，把他們毒啞並禁錮於自己家中，Michael 便是其中一個受害者了。

但我沒有不滿 • 148
主角身處的地方可能是戰火地區，或是因核輻射洩漏導致大規模死傷、糧食短缺。主角雖然命不久矣，但仍很知足，跟家人度過最後一個生日。

警力私有化 • 150
諷刺科技發展導致人性倒退，打電話報警也要聽錄音，甚至要收費，體現了「法律面前，窮人含忍」。

日食緊急指引 • 151
呼應 2017 年 8 月 21 日橫跨全美國的「超級全日食」。在日食期間走到戶外可能會感染不知名病毒，但是政府的呼籲可能已經太遲了。

前屋主的信 • 153
房子內有某種詛咒，會「奪去」兒童，而主角即將出生的孩子，就會成為這間屋下一個犧牲品。

極端妄想

Baxter 不認得我了 • 158
Baxter 是真的不認識主角，因為他是個入侵者，還妄想自己跟 Michelle 同住。

隱形的自己 • 161
小 A 到底只是主角的幻想，還是其實小 A 是找主角當替死鬼呢？

我缺席了母親的喪禮 • 164
主角害怕是自己開的槍令母親死亡，所以他寧願讓事實一直懸空，也不去看報告。

我女兒沒有離家出走 • 166
Katy 根本不是主角的女兒，因為主角是個人販子，把 Katy 抓回自己的家，還自欺說 Katy 安全回家了。

痴呆症與筷子 • 167
料理枱上的中式晚餐，有可能是入侵者想進駐主角家的徵兆，也可能是已故的爸爸幫忙買回來的。

請殺掉我 • 169
主角是隻狼人，與狼人習性相反，月圓反而會從狼變成人類，受人類價值觀束縛，但只要月圓結束，牠就可以繼續無憂無慮地生活了。

獨自在家 • 172
室友離開了但主角沒有不安感，是不是有甚麼東西陪著他呢？

他是該死的 • 173
主角一直以為院子裏的 Chris 是內疚感作祟，直至妹妹提及，才發現原來 Chris 是真的存在，不是幻覺。

捉迷藏 • 175
到底面前像喪屍的弟弟只是幻覺，還是在遠處倒數著的那個才是冒牌貨呢？

嗒嗒嗒 • 177
故事描述了人們的恐懼可能只是源於自己嚇自己，事實根本沒有可怕的東西。

Atum Beckett	CommanderSection
Ben Asper (DoverHawk)	Dave Fawkes
Brad VanHook	E. K. Riddle
Brittany Miller	Eliza Ferguson
Bryce Zayne	Gabriel Oro
Casey Cassetty	Heyward Hodges
Claudia Winters	J. A. Marshall

Jack T. Anderson

Nicholas Ong

James Marie Parker III

Noah Mester

Jeremy C. North

P. F. McGrail

Jerimi Galligory

Robert Wright

Kelly Childress

Sandi Kennedy

Kristopher Mallory

T. Ku

Laura L. Mack

V. R. Gregg

Thank you for providing creative and breathtaking stories.
Thank you for making the book enjoyable and relatable.

BOOK OF NO SLEEP
無眠書2

作者
Author

Short Scary Stories 版區作者
Short Scary Stories Authors

譯者
Translator

陳婉婷
Mia CHAN

出版總監
Publishing Director

余禮禧
Jim YU

特約編輯
Contributing Editor

羅慧詠
Venus LAW

美術設計
Designer

王子淇
Katie WONG

設計助理
Assistant Designer

郭海敏
Winny KWOK

製作
Producer

點子出版
Idea Publication

出版
Publisher

點子出版
Idea Publication

地址
Address

荃灣海盛路 11 號 One MidTown 13 樓 20 室
Unit 20, 13/F, One MidTown,
11 Hoi Shing Road, Tsuen Wan

查詢
Inquiry

info@idea-publication.com

發行
Distributor

泛華發行代理有限公司
Global China Circulation & Distribution Ltd

地址
Address

將軍澳工業邨駿昌街 7 號 2 樓
2/F ,7 Chun Cheong St,
Tseung Kwan O Industrial Estate

查詢
Inquiry

gccd@singtaonewscorp.com

出版日期
Publication Date

2022-7-20（第四版）

國際書碼
ISBN

978-988-77958-8-9

定價
Fixed Price

HKD$98

點子出版
IDEA PUBLICATION

BOOK OF NO SLEEP

無眠書2